Victim

Damaged Devils #16

Charity Parkerson

Punk & Sissy Publications

Copyright

—Warning: This book is intended for readers over the age of 18. Some of my

CHARITY PARKERSON

books contain allusions to past abuse and trauma.

CONTENTS

INTRODUCTION

DISILLUSIONED BY HIS JOB **with the FBI, Cannon is ready to make a change. He just never expects what the future has in store for him.**

After years of bureaucracy and playing by the rules, Cannon is at the end of his rope. He's seen behind the curtain where money matters more than the law. Cannon is done caring. He's followed all the procedures and danced to everyone's demands, playing the perfect agent. Now, he doesn't care. Let the world burn. He'll still take that paycheck, though. Cannon is owed that. When he finally goes too far and finds himself in the hot seat, Cannon has no intention of giving them the satisfaction of seeing him squirm. He's done being their victim. They have no idea what they've unleashed.

Xan isn't exactly on the right side of the law. Well, that depends on who a person asks. Some days, he runs a secret CIA program, negotiating eliminations. Other days, he liaisons between crime lords, killers, and the highest offices in the land. Someone has to do the dirty work. Cannon's prior dogged determination turned ticking time bomb is a problem he can't ignore. He has to get the guy out of the way before he blows a whole lot of people's lives out of the water. Xan just doesn't expect Cannon to be quite so cooperative... or irresistible.

Victim is the sixteenth book in Charity Parkerson's Damaged Devils series. These are dark romance stories with crime lords, assassins, and sociopaths who find their hearts. They are best enjoyed when read in order.

Author Note

THIS IS A DARK romance series filled with possible triggers. If you need a list, you can skip to the content warning after the About the Author page or check my website: charityparkerson.com/damaged-devils

Chapter One

Everything had a surreal edge. It had been that way since Cannon started non-stop drinking a few months back. He squinted at his computer screen, trying to read the blurry words. This was the first time he had been in the office in weeks. Unfortunately, he had to get this report done. He couldn't get his eyes to work properly. Since learning his job was pointless, Cannon had given up trying too hard. Money ruled the world and everything he did mattered not at all. As long as some rich white guy had the funds and connections, Cannon was just a useless puppet, which led him back to the computer screen swimming. He sipped his spiked coffee. Maybe another drink would straighten things out. He moved closer to the screen.

Since saying fuck it to his career, Cannon had recognized all the ways he had been dumb over the years. Why had he worked so hard? He should have been riding out this gravy train paycheck all along. His recent case was surveilling a known drug house. Cannon was supposed to be sitting outside each day. However, he had discovered he could set up a camera, record the place, and then quickly fast forward through the recordings each morning. That gave him just enough info to make a half-ass report. That method had bought him three weeks of lounging on his couch and drinking. He was oddly into a soap opera he had discovered. After this report was finished, Cannon planned to see if he could push it to six weeks this next time. His shows were set to record for the day, and he didn't think anyone would notice his absence. It wasn't like anything he did made a difference anyhow. They were all just playing at being law enforcers. Cannon might as well get to enjoy his free government money. This was the life. No responsibilities. A check kept getting deposited into his bank account. The alcohol kept flowing. Cannon got to pretend he didn't know more than half the people under this roof were on the take. Everything worked out for everyone involved.

The phone rang on his desk. Cannon blinked at it. He didn't think—as long as he had worked for the FBI—that phone had ever rung. Cannon hadn't even known it worked. It rang again. Cannon lifted the receiver to his ear.

"Whitley."

"Your ass, in my office, now!"

A dial tone buzzed in his ear. Cannon swore he heard his boss, Jake Hamilton, slamming down his handset from all the way down the hall. Cannon blew out a sigh. It looked like he didn't have six more weeks, after all. That was too bad. He kind of enjoyed getting paid to do nothing. Plus, he really wanted to know if Amanda ended up with Scott and if he ever found out she carried Edmund's baby. Damn. Looked like he would have to keep recording the show. He took another drink before bothering to head that way. Cannon pushed to his feet and measured each step. He was getting pretty good at pretending to be sober. Cannon had been practicing. He didn't bother knocking when he got to Jake's office.

Jake looked up as he entered the room. His face was set in a permanent frown. Cannon imagined he was close to sixty. Maybe older, but there were no laugh lines around his eyes. His hair was mostly gray. It was possible this job had just aged him. He stared at Cannon with angry dark brown eyes, as if he expected Cannon to know why he was there. Cannon figured he knew, but he would be damned if he admitted to anything. He wasn't invited to sit. Cannon imagined that was part of the psychological games.

Jake broke first. "Why haven't I gotten anything from you on the Kingston Street house? That place is responsible for putting more fentanyl-laced drugs on the street than any other place in Alabama. We need to know who their supplier is, but I don't see any damn reports on my desk."

Cannon shrugged. "I was just working on it." He also felt like this was a case for the DEA, but whatever. It had landed on his lap.

"Give me the cliff notes."

Cannon bit back a sigh. "There's only been the same three cars in and out of there in the past few weeks. I've already given all the details to the local PD—without telling them why we're on the lookout, of course—and I've entered it into the national database. So far, no high-level players have made an appearance."

Jake didn't look impressed. "That's it? Three fucking weeks and that's all you have. You're supposed to be a better agent than this. We need that supplier."

Cannon's drunk mouth chose a sober mind. "Why? As soon as it turns out to be some rich guy with connections, I'll be told to drop it. So why are we wasting my time and taxpayer money?"

Jake's eye twitched. Cannon knew he had gone too far, but they both knew Jake was on the take. He was oddly curious to see how Jake would react.

"Quentin Montgomery was clean." Jake said the words between clenched teeth.

There it was—the reason Cannon had given up. Cannon had spent months investigating Quentin and his so-called family. The guy had purchased several men from an underground program that tortured children, turning them into monsters. They were sold to the highest bidder and set loose on society. These men killed indiscriminately, yet Quentin had purchased several people from the organization. Quentin got away with it because he had the kind of money that went back so far and wide, it couldn't be traced. That was it. Money ruled the world and Cannon had to dance to its tune.

Cannon snorted so hard, it hurt. "Quentin Montgomery is free because it suits you and we both know it. This country has turned a blind eye to literal human trafficking because it serves us to do so. These programs churn out men we can use to our advantage and keep our hands clean in the process, but our hands aren't clean, any more than Quentin's, and you know it. But I suppose you're getting enough money under the table to un-know it." As soon as the words left his lips, Cannon knew his career was over. There was no going back. Everything he felt for the past few months lingered between them now.

Jake released a tired-sounding sigh. "One week suspension. Leave your badge and gun." He went back to working on his computer as if the matter was settled and Cannon's opinion meant nothing. Really, it didn't. It wasn't like anyone would believe him about this crooked organization. If they did, it still didn't matter. The corruption went all the way to the top. His thoughts mattered not at all.

Cannon didn't argue. Honestly, he was more than a little surprised he wasn't fired. It was whatever, though. His career had been over since they fired him and rehired him two months ago, just to prove how little control he had. Cannon had just been playing his part, trying to milk as much money from the government as he could before returning to civilian life. He left his gun and badge and headed for the door. Jake hadn't said anything about his suspension being unpaid, so that was awesome. Cannon could use an unexpected week off. It gave him a chance to do one of his favorite things: stalk his ex.

Xan stared at the nondescript Camry where Cannon sat, watching his ex's place. That was truly where the issue began. Xan ran a CIA team and worked as a liaison between former society and academy graduates who did freelance work for the government. Basically, he green lit sanctioned off the books murders the U.S. didn't want associated with them. Ah, the land of the free. Terms and conditions applied, of course. Capitalism at its finest. Unfortunately, Cannon's ex was engaged to one of the men Xan had on murder speed dial to do his bidding. This stalking business was ridiculous, honestly. From Xan's research, it looked as if Cannon had been given all the time in the world to do right by Knight. Instead, he had waited until Knight fell for Royal to become this obsessed. The dumbass. Double unfortunately, Cannon had officially gone too far. Now Xan had to get involved. The country had to protect itself, after all. Who better to call than a Russian-born orphan who had gone from an assassination program to climb to one of the highest positions in the CIA. The American dream.

Xan slid from the car that had given him a ride. He thanked the agent behind the wheel and then made his way to Cannon's driver's side door. He was more than a little surprised Cannon didn't see him coming. Cannon startled as Xan jerked open the door.

"What the fuck?" When Cannon realized it was him, his expression changed, turning guilty. "Oh. Hey. What are you doing here? Are you stalking too?" A nervous laugh escaped Cannon.

"Get out."

Cannon climbed from the car. The scent of alcohol overwhelmed him. "Like, do you want to fight or something...? I'm retired Special Forces, you know. I won't be that easy to take."

Xan rolled his eyes. He crowded Cannon's space, letting Cannon see his annoyance. "Get in the passenger seat."

Cannon looked more than a little confused, but he did as instructed. Xan slid behind the wheel. He didn't have to adjust the seat and mirrors the way he usually did. Cannon matched his six feet in height. In fact, they were built almost exactly the same.

The moment Cannon buckled his seat-belt, Xan pulled away from the curb. "I hear you've decided to tank your career."

Cannon snorted. It was a bitter sound. "What career? Do you mean being a puppet for the highest bidder? That's not a career. That's a joke."

Xan fought another eye roll. "Being a drunkard doesn't suit you. Right now, it's making you look dumb as fuck. As retired Special Forces, you should know damn well some people are better off dead. Sometimes, you have to do what's necessary for the greater good."

"I'm not a drunk. I'm coping." Cannon sounded almost childish. "One of your fucking barely leashed animals is living under my friend's roof. There's nothing stopping him from having some sort of meltdown and hurting Knight. I need to make sure that doesn't happen."

Xan lost the battle against another eye roll. "Knight is perfectly fine. In fact, he's pretty fucking happy. Just because Royal is marrying Knight and Knight won't be sucking your dick any longer, that's not the FBI or the CIA's fault. That's Cannon Lee Whitley's fault. Get the fuck over it, stop sucking your mom's tit, and find someone else."

"They're getting married?"

At the quietly spoken question, Xan shot a quick glance Cannon's way. "I thought you knew since you've been acting like a crazy person."

"No. I didn't know." A moment of silence passed. Cannon cleared his throat. "So, where are we headed anyway? Am I being kidnapped?"

Xan shrugged. "If you want to look at it that way, yes. The bureau has decided you need some time on ice to readjust your thoughts and dry out. You've just recently visited your parents and you're three months away from your birthday. You have no significant other. I imagine, since your parents are likely used to losing contact with you when you're undercover, no one will even notice you're missing for several months. That gives you plenty of time to reorganize your priorities."

A soft, uncomfortably sexy chuckle rumbled from Cannon's side of the car. "You're not very good at this kidnapping thing. You didn't check my pockets. I still have my phone. All I have to do is call for help."

An evil smile stretched Xan's lips. "Do you, though? Still have your phone, that is."

Cannon shifted as if to dig his phone from his pocket. "What the fuck? Where's my phone?"

Xan held up the phone he had lifted from Cannon's pocket earlier. Drunk men were easy to rob. "This phone?" Xan rolled down the window and threw it out.

Cannon twisted in his seat. "What the fuck, dude?" Xan could feel Cannon's enraged stare boring into him. "Fine. I'll just get out at the next light."

Xan laughed. He was enjoying himself more than he should. Xan intentionally slowed, so he was forced to stop at the next light. "Do it then."

Cannon grabbed the door handle. Nothing happened. "I can shout for help." He tried rolling down the window. Nothing happened.

Xan's face hurt from smiling. He tapped the panel on the driver's side door. "Child locks."

Fury filled eyes focused on him. "I'm still retired Special Forces. I'm not as weak as you seem to think." He moved to attack.

Xan easily caught his fist and twisted. He released Cannon before he did any real damage.

Cannon shook out his wrist.

The light turned green. Xan let his foot off the brake. "Suck it up, buttercup. This is happening. You may as well sit back and enjoy the ride."

For a moment, no sound came from Cannon's side of the car. He shook his wrist a couple of more times. After a second, unexpected laughter rumbled from Cannon. "You said suck it up, buttercup." He laughed harder. "In a Russian accent."

Xan shook his head, fighting a smile. It was too bad Cannon was such a bitter and pious asshole. He was kind of fun.

CHAPTER TWO

XAN NEVER TRIED HIDING where they were. There was no point. It was a safe house in the middle of nowhere. If he left on foot, he wouldn't die before he found the nearest town, but he would probably wish he had. Not to mention, the land was covered with cameras and silent alarms. The second he ran for it, he would have a hundred agents from every alphabet crawling up his asshole.

Cannon threw himself down on the couch and grabbed the remote. If he was here for the long haul, he may as well enjoy his time off. If he logged into his account, he could watch his shows from here.

Xan's light blue gaze followed his every move, obviously mistrusting his acceptance. "I packed you a bag earlier. It's in the bedroom."

"All right. I hope you packed comfortable clothes since I'm just chilling."

"You'll make do, I'm sure."

Exhaustion washed over Cannon. The alcohol was wearing off, and he needed a nap. "How long is this timeout?"

Xan shrugged as he sat in the recliner. "That depends on you. Once you get sober and stop endangering the lives of my agents, we'll talk."

That bunched Cannon's briefs. "Your *agents* are a bunch of ruthless murderers trained to have zero conscience. The animals you claim Quentin 'saved' are no more than that: animals. They should've been put down before being allowed to mingle in society. If Quentin Montgomery wasn't rich with powerful connections, that's what would've happened. When Royal has some sort of PTSD breakdown and goes on a killing spree, I'll be right there saying my I told you so's. I just pray Knight isn't caught in the crossfire." The topic had Cannon fired up again. He was the only person to see these academy and society members for the monsters they were. Cannon wasn't unaware these men had been tortured in ways he could never fathom. He wasn't unfeeling to that. But the kind thing would have been to take them out. Quentin Montgomery hadn't rescued anyone. He had trafficked monsters into the country.

Xan didn't respond for a minute. Cannon thought the conversation had ended. Then Xan spoke in a quiet voice that sent chills down Cannon's spine. "I'm one of those animals Quentin rescued. Considering my record for keeping this country safe, you should be grateful no one 'put me down.' It's not Quentin, his money, or powerful friends that shut down the investigation against him. It was me. Maybe you should look deeper into things before you run your fucking mouth, because you know nothing about *me*."

Xan was right. Cannon knew nothing about the guy beyond his exemplary record and his unquestionable authority. So Xan wasn't totally correct. Someone powerful had shut down Quentin's case. Nonetheless, he hadn't known Xan was one of Quentin's rescues. That definitely gave him something to think about. He just hadn't decided if his thoughts should be on reconsidering his stance or plotting his escape from a monster. Either way, he still wasn't sober enough to make a rational decision. Maybe after his nap. It had been a hell of a day.

Xan's shoulders didn't relax until Cannon finally slept. He waffled between rage and sadness. It had taken him years to deprogram from nearly a decade of being tortured into submission. Now he did his best to offer a new path for people like him. Unfortunately, people like Cannon existed. In a small way, Cannon wasn't completely wrong. Not everyone like Xan and Royal could be saved. More people than not left those assassin programs more beast than man. They were unfixable. But they were still people who were once tortured children, and they deserved the chances that had been stolen from them. There was a deep passion inside Xan about the topic. People like Cannon could never understand. Cannon had led an unblemished life with two parents and a dog when he was a child. He'd had everything Xan had prayed to have. Yet he turned out to be a judgmental asshole with zero empathy and a drinking problem. It was as irritating as it was disheartening. Xan would never be good enough to exist in Cannon's eyes. That made him want to punch a hole in the wall.

With a sigh, Xan headed inside the bedroom he would enjoy while Cannon figured out his next steps. Either he would get sober and smarter, or one of them would end up dead. Xan hated that for the man's parents, because it sure as hell wouldn't be Xan who ended up six feet under, but the final decision would be Cannon's. Xan couldn't make him wake up to reality. This was how the world worked. Cannon should know that by now. Adapt or die.

After a hot shower, Xan found a pair of workout shorts and a tank top. He might as well be comfortable while babysitting. When he finally emerged from his room, he found Cannon angrily rummaging through the cabinets.

Cannon shot him an annoyed look. "You're keeping me hostage in a house with no food."

While keeping his gaze locked on Cannon, Xan opened the nearby bread box and grabbed the bread. He set it on the counter before opening the fridge and finding ham and cheese. He slapped them down on the counter. "Food."

Cannon rolled his eyes. "No good food," he muttered under his breath. Despite his protest, he unwound the twist tie on the bread.

Xan pulled a stool out from the island and sat. "Not everyone grew up spoiled like you."

Cannon released a long, drawn out, and obnoxious sigh. "I'm not spoiled. I've been taken against my will. At the very least, I should be allowed some decent food."

"Make a list and we'll get it delivered. We may as well enjoy Uncle Sam's money."

"Do you want a sandwich?" Cannon sounded gruff. He didn't look at Xan as he made the offer.

Xan recognized it for the olive branch it was. "Sure."

With a nod, he slapped together a sandwich for Xan before digging condiments from the fridge. He set them and two cans of soda on the island before grabbing another bar stool and joining Xan.

Cannon took a bite. He eyed the place as if he didn't want to meet Xan's stare. That gave Xan the freedom to watch him. He always had tanned skin, which—along with his dark hair—made his amber eyes pop. The guy made him curious.

"Do you go to the tanning bed or stay at the pool? I've never seen you without a tan."

A smile exploded across Cannon's face. He chuckled. "This is my natural skin col-

or. My mom is Mexican. You didn't know that?"

Xan shook his head. "Why would I know that?"

Cannon shrugged. "I assumed you knew every detail of my life."

He decided he should be honest. "Truthfully, I got a basic rundown. From the way your parents were described, I assumed they were backwoods Baptists who hate anyone the least bit different from them."

Cannon set his unfinished sandwich aside. He wiped his hands on his pants as he chewed. Finally, he swallowed. "Maybe in some ways they are those people. Except my dad served in the military, and—well—I started to say you know how that is, but I guess you don't. It's impossible to hate someone different when that person has your six. They're your brothers and sisters. Unfortunately, that's where his tolerance stops. If something challenges his religious beliefs, then you can hear the change in his voice. You can hear the scathing when he talks about refusing to condone anyone's sins by accepting them."

"Like being gay."

Cannon nodded, but he didn't look at Xan. "Like being gay."

"No wonder you're an alcoholic."

Cannon made a sound between a scoff and a sigh. "I'm not an alcoholic. I've already told you I'm just coping right now. Are you telling me you have zero bad habits to deal with the bullshit known as life? Do you just wake up in the morning, kiss your dog on the mouth, and throw the window open to greet the day?"

Damn. Cannon was bitter as fuck. "I don't have a dog."

Cannon shook his head. He held Xan's stare, like he was genuinely baffled. "After the life you've lived, you're saying you're totally square with existence?"

The tiny island where they sat was the only line between the ridiculously small kitchen and living room. The two-bedroom cabin was just that. A hunting cabin. It wasn't meant for full-time living. Xan easily turned and grabbed his suit jacket from the recliner where he left it, since it was only inches away. He patted the pockets until he pulled out a white box and a lighter. Xan shook out a slim cigar and lit it. The laced smoke barely affected him anymore.

He held it out to Cannon. "How I cope."

To his surprise, Cannon accepted. After a singular drag, he coughed. "Holy shit. No way are you passing our in-depth drug testing."

Xan laughed. "I've surpassed the level of random testing. Plus, I have a special set of skills. They're not hiring just anyone to replace me." Xan reclaimed his cigar and took another two puffs. He held it out to Cannon again.

Since learning what it was, he fully expected Cannon to turn him down this time. He didn't.

Xan couldn't stop smiling. "I guess we'd best hope you're not up for any random tests."

Cannon shrugged. "I figure I'm done no matter what I do at this point. They don't want someone who rocks the boat. They only want mindless drones who follow orders without question."

"You were moving up the ranks of those mindless drones until you let yourself get thrown off track." They passed the cigar between them a few times before Cannon responded.

"I guess a part of me always knew I worked for a corrupt government. Each day, I just hoped we did more good than bad. I don't think I can say that anymore."

His mind took on a hint of haze and loosened Xan's tongue. "I don't think your problems have anything to do with the bureau."

Cannon snorted. "Pray tell. What is my problem?"

Xan shrugged. "You want to be free. When you look around, you see every-one else choosing happiness over rea-son. You want that too. But you don't see a path towards bliss. If you stay the course, you'll die alone, bitter, and likely drunk. If you choose the life you truly want, then maybe you lose your family." Xan shrugged again. "I don't have one of those, so I say, do as you please. But then, maybe if anyone had ever wanted me beyond a band of sadistic men, possibly I'd be scared to lose them too. I'll never know." He held the cigar out to Cannon. "Here. Finish this."

Cannon accepted. He looked unusually stoic. "I guess I should just be grateful for the amazing parents I was given and be forever alone."

Xan's face screwed up in confusion. "I don't know how amazing they are if they want that for you. But you could just find someone who doesn't give a fuck if they never meet your parents."

An unexpectedly sexy chuckle rumbled from Cannon. "There's no one out there like that."

A laugh burst from Xan. "That's not true. I'm like that. No way in hell do I want to be under any parents' microscope. That's an inspection I'm doomed to fail." Xan stood. He squeezed Cannon's shoulders as he moved past him. "Make that food list. I'll get everything brought out tomorrow. For now, I'm going to bed. Thanks for the sandwich."

Cannon nodded but didn't say anything. Xan scurried to the safety of his room before he admitted anything more about himself. Since there was no telling how long he would be stuck there, he had plenty of time to say more stupid things. With Cannon's attitude, they likely had weeks.

Chapter Three

Spending time with Xan turned out be a quiet peace Cannon didn't expect. The day after his abduction, Cannon found Xan doing his daily workout outside. Watching him made Cannon realize how lazy the use of gym equipment could be. He joined in and felt stronger than ever after only two weeks together. They watched TV, snacked, and played cards. Mostly, they just sat together. Cannon felt calmer than he had in a long time.

They built a fire in the backyard fire pit and sat together, watching the flames. It was like going on a work retreat where they took everyone's phone and forced them to reconnect with nature. Cannon had been deployed several times and gone on missions where there was nothing but various harsh natures. This was like a camping trip for him.

"I expected you to be a tougher hostage."

A laugh burbled in Cannon's throat. He looked Xan's way. Fire light danced on his features, making him look deadlier than usual. "That's because I don't give a fuck. It was the bureau's phone you threw out that car window. I've been due a vacation for years. When all this is said and done, I have no intention of returning to work, so." He shrugged. "I may as well eke out a few more weeks of pay from the government before I'm unemployed. Fuck them people. They mean less than nothing to me."

"Jake doesn't want you to quit. He knows you're an excellent agent. The bureau has plans for you."

"They just want me to look the other way and throw away every ounce of integrity for them. No thanks." Cannon went back to staring at the fire. "I already have too many crosses to bear and secrets to keep. I'm smart enough to know when to stop digging."

"You are smart," Xan said, surprising him. "You're intelligent enough to know nothing is black and white."

Cannon met Xan's stare again. "Why does this matter so much to you? When this is done, you'll kill me or discredit me to the point of ruin. Then you'll go on with your life like we never met. So why push? How I think and feel matters to absolutely no one. Why do you care if I keep my sense of what's right and what's wrong to the end?"

Xan looked away. He buried his hands in the pockets of his coat and slid down in his chair. His gaze stayed locked on the fire. "I suppose it doesn't matter. My whole adult life, I've dealt with pious snobs like you. You're right. I shouldn't care what you think of me."

Confusion ruled Cannon. "What are you talking about? We were discussing my career and what I can live with and what I can't. What in the hell does that have to do with you?"

Xan met his stare. Cannon lost his breath as he caught sight of a side of Xan he hadn't expected. The guy looked like a real person for once. Not the deadly weapon he was. "Everything you said about why you won't return to work is me. Your decision to walk away because of realizing people like Royal are funded by the government, that's me. I'm Royal. I'm what you think you're too good to sully your hands with." Xan stood. "Just forget it, okay? You've made your decision. I'll let Jake know where you stand." He walked away, leaving Cannon wondering what the fuck had just happened. They had been sitting here peacefully. Cannon thought they had come to somewhat of a silent camaraderie.

Cannon rubbed his forehead. Fuck. He wished he didn't feel the sting of Xan's words, but Xan was right. When Cannon stepped back and looked at everything he claimed, from an objective point of view, it sounded like he couldn't stand being lumped in with people like Xan—like he thought he was better and wouldn't sully his good name by working hand in hand with the likes of Xan. Goddamn it.

With a growl, Cannon stood. He doused the fire and followed Xan. Cannon didn't know what he could say to make Xan understand his side of things. His feelings had nothing to do with Xan's background. He was angry over the way the entire game was rigged for the rich. Cannon hated knowing he worked for people who would turn a blind eye to programs that tortured kids because, ultimately, they produced more people like

Xan for them to exploit. He couldn't be party to that. Cannon just wasn't good at expressing himself. He had too much pent-up resentment.

Once inside, Cannon headed straight for Xan's bedroom. He didn't knock. His mind was too preoccupied with trying to figure out the right words to use. "Listen, Xan." Cannon froze. Xan was shirtless, with his back to the door. He was nothing but scars. Cannon had caught sight of Xan shirtless from the front before, which was fucking per-fection. This was different. Cannon's stomach churned. Xan's back was just a roadmap of scarred-over untreated wounds. Cuts. Whip marks. Cigar burns. Gun-shot wounds.

Even though Xan immediately turned when he stormed the room, it was like it happened in slow motion. Cannon didn't miss a single mark. He couldn't breathe. Xan had a laced cigar hanging from his lips. His pants hung low on his hips. Sexy abs screamed for attention, trying to trick Cannon into forgetting what he had seen. His chest hurt. Xan had gotten those scars over the span of his childhood. A fucking child.

Suddenly, Cannon had all the words. "I don't think I'm above you. In fact, I think you're fucking amazing. Always have. My anger and bitterness aren't about you. It's for you. How can anyone ask me to go back and pledge my loyalty to people who knew you and others like you were suffering? They left you there because it suited their purposes to do so. That's what I can't live with."

Xan didn't respond. In fact, his expression never changed—like he was bored.

Cannon was too in his feelings. He felt too much passion for the career he thought he had been working. He thought he had been making a difference.

"How do you live with it?" Even Cannon heard the plea in his quietly spoken question.

Xan calmly snuffed out his cigar in the ashtray next to the bed. Cannon watched Xan cross the room. Before he saw it coming, Xan cupped his face and kissed him. It was arguably the hottest and most skilled kiss Cannon had ever experienced in his life. Unfortunately, Cannon didn't get to enjoy it as much as he would have liked, since he was so caught off guard. By the time his brain caught up with the moment, it was over.

Xan didn't release Cannon's face right away. He swiped the moisture from Cannon's bottom lip. "How do you live with giving up everything that makes you you to keep up appearances you hate? Everyone makes their choices."

Without another word, Xan turned away and closed himself inside his bathroom. Cannon stared at the closed door, trying to figure out what had just happened to his life.

Xan stared at himself in the mirror, wishing he hadn't left his cigar in the ashtray. His light blue eyes looked colder than usual. Maybe that was just him. He kept seeing the pleading in Cannon's eyes and comparing that to his empty stare. Cannon had passion. Fire. He believed in things. The guy had heart. Xan possessed none of that.

He dug his phone from his pocket. It had been two weeks. Xan couldn't say he hadn't tried. But Cannon's deep-seated feelings and stance on life couldn't and wouldn't be budged by time away from everything. Plus, the guy hadn't been lying. Cannon wasn't an alcoholic. Not a drop of the stuff had been in his body the past fourteen days, and there had been no change in Cannon signaling withdrawals. This was pointless.

X: *This is pointless. Move to Plan B.*

G: *Received and understood.*

Xan went back to staring at his reflection. His gaze dropped to his lips. Cannon's flavor still lingered there. He didn't know what had come over him. All Cannon's passion had been directed at him, showing more pain and outrage on Xan's behalf than anyone else ever had. An overwhelming need to taste that zeal had overcome him. That kiss had been way more amazing than he could have imagined. Damn. That was a shame. He genuinely liked Cannon. Despite Cannon's over-the-top sanctimonious attitude about life, Xan actually enjoyed his company. Cannon brought a quiet peace to the room, broken by bursts of humor. None of that mattered any longer. His text was sent, received, and understood. It was over. He had failed in his mission. Now he had to pay the price.

CHAPTER FOUR

CANNON HAD LAIN AWAKE way too long, thinking about that kiss. He peeked out his bedroom window to make sure he didn't miss a workout with Xan. Xan was nowhere to be seen. Disappointment hit. He started the shower. Throughout his shower, Cannon zoned out. Why had Xan kissed him? Was it just to prove a point? Fuck. It had been an amazing kiss. Goddamn it. Cannon wanted to do it again. He had always recognized Xan was gorgeous. Blond hair, blue eyes, cut jaw and body. Who wouldn't think he was perfect? But Cannon's ass was always on the line with Xan. Cannon just hadn't looked at him in that light. Now, he couldn't stop.

He dragged his feet through his morning routine. Cannon wasn't sure he was ready to face Xan just yet. There was no avoiding it. With a breath for strength, Cannon opened his bedroom door and froze. The front door hung from its hinges. The place was trashed. A trail of blood led out the front door. Cannon's heart stopped and started again. Xan's bedroom door stood open. From Cannon's vantage point, he could see the room torn to bits. Blood splattered the white comforter. Cannon's feet moved faster than his brain. He raced through the cabin and burst into the room. All Xan's things were scattered. His phone was on the floor. There was blood everywhere. Cannon turned in a circle. His mind raced. He headed for the busted front door. If there was any chance Xan was outside, fighting for his life, Cannon needed to find him. As he cleared the doorway, a sea of black SUVs poured into the driveway. Agents spilled out. Cannon's mind couldn't keep up with the shocks. Then he spotted a familiar face. His old partner, Gable, who had been promoted a few years back, led the pack. He carried a black backpack. As he climbed the porch steps, he passed the bag Cannon's way.

"We got here as soon as we could. The perimeter alarm alerted us as soon as the area was breached. That's your gear. Jake wants you in charge of this."

All Cannon could do was blink. "I don't even know what happened. The place is trashed, and I didn't hear a thing."

Gable didn't react, as if he wasn't surprised. "Did you have anything to drink last night?"

Cannon shook his head, and then he remembered something. He had snatched the cigar Xan had left behind and finished it. Fuck. He had been high as hell by the time he finally passed out. Cannon had to turn the questioning away from him. "Tell me what you know so far." Cannon listened while pulling his gear from the bag. His gun, badge, handcuffs, a new phone, and a bullet-proof vest were inside. He geared up, getting ready to do whatever it took as soon as possible.

"From what we picked up on camera, five men burst through the door two hours ago. A few minutes later, they dragged out a visibly unconscious Xan. All the men were dressed in black, keeping their identities hidden, but the man waiting behind the wheel hadn't covered his face." Gable produced a tablet. He pulled up a still shot. "This is Fediz Sidorov. He's from the same Russian society as Xan. His people have thrown around several threats over the years. They believe Xan has fed society information to the government."

Cannon studied the face. "They waited a long time to take him."

Gable shrugged. "Normally, Xan is sur-rounded by agents. Out here, I suppose they thought he was vulnerable. They thought wrong. As you know, every inch of this place is wired."

Cannon met Gable's stare. "You know where they've taken him." It wasn't a question. They both knew someone as high up as Xan couldn't disappear from the planet. Cannon wouldn't be surprised if they had him chipped like a dog.

An evil-looking smile stretched Gable's lips. "We know where they've taken him."

Cannon checked his weapon to ensure it was fully loaded before shoving into its holster. "Okay. I want three teams. You come with me. I need you to fill me in on every inch of where he's being kept along the way." They headed for the nearest SUV. Cannon could quit tomorrow. Today, he had to save his friend.

Everything hurt. Xan measured each breath. Nothing was broken, but he was definitely bruised. While Xan had been built for this abuse, it had—admittedly—been a while since he had taken a beating. His wrists were raw from the ropes binding his wrists. The taste of blood filled his mouth. He ran his tongue across his teeth, checking them one by one. It seemed the blood came from his teeth, cutting into his lips. He was good. Xan could handle this.

He eyed his surroundings. The warehouse had a ton of dust lingering in the air. He fought to keep his eyes open. Xan was getting too old to be up all night, getting his ass handed to him. From his angle, Xan could see inside an open doorway. It looked to be an old break room. Six men surrounded a table, drinking and playing cards. Yeah. He should have finished that cigar last night. Maybe then he could find a halfway comfortable spot to sleep while tied to a chair. Damn. He had forgotten how badly this sucked. America had made him soft.

A loud boom sent the men scrambling. Agents poured through the door, led by Cannon. Fuck. He looked hot. In his element. For all his drinking and bitching, he hadn't lost his game. His face was set in hard lines as he crossed the warehouse, heading Xan's way. Agents watched his back, taking down and handcuffing Xan's kidnappers. Xan never looked away from Cannon. The man had been born to do this job.

With his weapon sweeping from side to side, as Cannon watched for danger, the distance between them disappeared. Cannon dropped to one knee. He set his gun aside and went to work on Xan's binds.

"You can thank me for rescuing your ass later."

A laugh burst from Xan at the humor in Cannon's voice. The guy was clearly enjoying himself. He lived for this job. "Fuck you. If you didn't sleep like the goddamn dead, I wouldn't be in this position."

Cannon's laughing gaze focused on Xan. "What? You couldn't handle six guys alone? Weak."

Xan couldn't look away from Cannon. This was the real him. Happy. Brave. "I guess your job has some legit days, after all. You get to call yourself my hero."

Cannon shook his head, but he didn't stop smiling. With Xan's ropes gone, Cannon grabbed his weapon and moved back to his feet. "Can you walk?"

"Other than my ass being asleep, yeah."

Cannon still helped him to his feet. He searched Xan for injuries. "What did the guys hope to gain by this?"

"Money. Isn't it always about money? I suppose they think the U.S. owes them payment for my services." He dipped his chin, ensuring Cannon met his stare. Xan needed him to understand this part because Cannon didn't get it. "People like me. We're never free. Not really. These people see us as property they can reclaim at any moment. There's not a single one of us who wouldn't die before we went back."

Cannon didn't react. "Your leg is bleeding. Lean on me until we're out of here and I can get a better look at your injuries."

Xan bit back a sigh and draped his arm over Cannon's shoulders. Cannon didn't want to soften at the idea of Xan's team. He was so fucking set in his ways. Together, they made their way toward the door. Xan glanced toward the six men on their stomachs with their hands behind their backs.

Cannon followed his gaze. He pointed toward Gable. "I want to talk to these guys. I have questions."

Gable made a dismissive gesture. "Worry about him right now. You can question these guys later. They're not going anywhere."

With a nod, Cannon helped Xan outside to a waiting SUV. Xan opened the door and sat sideways across the passenger seat. Cannon put his rifle in the backseat before returning to inspect Xan's leg.

"There was so much blood back at the cabin, I didn't know what I would find."

Xan nodded and lifted his shirt. "Yeah. One of those bastards stabbed me."

Cannon immediately jumped into action. "Why didn't you say something sooner? I'll get you a medic."

Xan waved off the suggestion. He had known his black shirt hid the damage. "It's fine. They just grazed me. I've had much worse."

The exasperation in Cannon's expression was almost comical. "It's not about what you can handle. It's about your health."

"I'm good." Cannon's concern moved him more than Xan cared to admit. His hands landed on Cannon's hips. It was out of his control. The way Cannon looked bursting through that door still lingered in his mind. "You saved me."

Cannon shuffled closer. "Well, despite everything, you're not a complete ass."

He shuffled even closer. "Plus, I couldn't let you die until you answered a question that's driving me crazy."

"What's that?"

"Why did you kiss me?" Cannon didn't blush. He was completely straightforward.

"For the same reason I plan to do so again, because I want to." He hauled Cannon forward and claimed his mouth. It hurt. Fuck, it hurt. Cuts lined the inside of his mouth, forcing him to keep things short. Plus, they could get caught at any second. Xan didn't care, but Cannon likely did.

Cannon pulled away, looking sexy and aroused. It took his breath. "Damn. That had to hurt. Maybe heal a little before you try again."

A smirk pulled at Xan's lips. Oh, it would happen again. Xan could guarantee that.

CHAPTER FIVE

AS BADLY AS CANNON wanted to slam heads into walls and beat some answers from Xan's abductors, Xan looked tired as hell. No doubt he had been kept awake the entire time, wearing down his resistance. The men were in custody. Cannon could question them tomorrow. As Gable had said, they weren't going anywhere. Cannon didn't ask where he could take Xan. He simply drove back to the cabin, retrieved his car, and went home. Xan didn't argue, which either proved Cannon's suspension and ice time were up or Xan was just too tired to fight.

With the shock and adrenaline gone, Cannon had more questions than answers. Why had Jake chosen him to lead the operation to rescue Xan? Was it an olive branch? Cannon was the expert in hostage retrieval. He had led more successful missions in that area than any other agent. Looking at things clinically, he had been the best choice. Something just felt weird about the entire situation. Xan was CIA. That made the operation multi-divisional. They could have chosen anyone. Maybe he was simply still off kilter from Xan's kiss. With zero cockiness, Cannon was the perfect choice to lead the team. That was all.

As they pulled into Cannon's garage, Cannon explained, even though Xan hadn't asked and the situation seemed obvious. "You'll stay with me. At least until you're rested. Gable has your things. Your phone, wallet, keys, and whatnot," he clarified. "He'll drop everything off after he oversees suspect transport."

"Sounds good."

Cannon looked Xan's way. He could barely hold his eyes open. Cannon slid from the car and circled to Xan's side. He opened the door. "Come on. Let's get you inside and cleaned up so you can sleep."

Xan let Cannon help him through the door. His two-bedroom condo had two bathrooms. Each one was inside a bedroom. He had thought to let Xan have the guest room slash home gym, but there were no toiletries in the guest bathroom. Not only had Cannon rarely been home before the FBI fallout, but he also didn't have anyone in his life to stay overnight. He didn't have friends. Depression washed over Cannon as he headed for his bedroom. This job had really stolen everything from him. What his long hours and secret missions hadn't taken, Cannon had lost by being too scared to come out as gay. He wasn't dumb. Cannon knew he had thrown himself into work, becoming the best, just so he could avoid slowing down enough to fix his life. He couldn't change who he was. This was how he had been born. That didn't make it any easier. His family was also who they were. He saw no middle ground.

Inside his bathroom, Cannon put down the lid on the toilet seat so Xan could sit. With Xan settled, he got the shower going. While the water heated, Cannon gently peeled off Xan's shirt. If the material had glued to any bloody wounds, Cannon didn't want to tear anything open.

"You don't have to do this. I'm tougher than I look right now." He visibly hesitated. "Plus, I know how my body looks."

Cannon wouldn't have taken Xan for a man who possessed a single insecurity. He went down on one knee and helped Xan with his socks. "How do you look? Like a guy who takes amazing care of himself," Cannon supplied. "Or do you mean the way your body proves your mental strength?" Cannon met his stare. "Never be ashamed of surviving where other people would've quit. I know how you look too, and I think you're sexy as fuck."

If his words made Xan feel any way at all, Cannon would never know. Xan was the master of hiding his thoughts behind a smooth mask. The guy had been tortured into an emotionless killer. Cannon didn't doubt hiding his feelings was a survival instinct. Cannon couldn't fix him. He couldn't even fix himself.

Cannon shifted back to his feet. "Do you think you can handle showering, or do you need my help?"

"My pride would love to claim I'm fine, but my energy is zapped. Unfortunately, I also know if you get in that shower with me, I'll make you uncomfortable as hell. There's no way I can shower with you and not get hard, exhausted or not. I think you're sexy as fuck too."

Cannon didn't have Xan's training. He couldn't hide his emotions. A smile exploded across his face. "That's okay. Likely I'll be hard too. I'm strong enough to handle it without molesting you."

A small, tired-looking smile touched Xan's lips. "The mind is willing, but my body doesn't have the strength."

A soft chuckle escaped Cannon. "It's all good. I'm pretty fucking tired too. Let's get clean and crash."

Xan nodded. It was beyond obvious he wouldn't last much longer. Cannon stripped, trying not to think too much about the situation. He didn't possess an ounce of modesty. Years in the military and similar situations had stripped any semblance of embarrassment from him. Too many times to count, he had been given no other choice but to perform every private act very publicly. At some point, he had forgotten to care. When he was nude, he helped Xan out of the remainder of his clothes. Cannon tried to be clinical about it. This was almost medical care. Xan was his patient.

He steered Xan beneath the hot water and went to work. There was a basket of clean wash cloths sitting outside the shower. Cannon ran through a few of them, cleaning Xan's wounds. For the most part, they were pretty superficial. The one on his side probably needed to be glued closed. Cannon would do that after they were clean. He tried not to eye Xan's body. As promised, they were hard. It was unavoidable. There was obviously an attraction between them. They were nude and touching. It was just a normal human response. Cannon tried to be logical about the situation. Still, he avoided Xan's gaze. He was afraid of what Xan might see in his eyes.

Cannon gently washed Xan's hair before quickly doing his own. He efficiently scrubbed their bodies and rinsed their skin. He killed the water and grabbed a fluffy towel that hung from a nearby hook. Cannon took care of Xan first. Once he had him completely dry, Cannon wrapped the towel around his hips and led Xan to his bed.

"Sit. I need to grab the first aid kit and glue that cut closed before you fall asleep. Otherwise, you'll end up sticking to the sheets and tearing it open the first time you move."

Xan nodded.

Cannon hurried. Xan's eyelids were drooping. He was going down fast. As soon as he had the wound glued, he urged Xan onto his back and covered him. "Sleep."

With Xan settled, Cannon moved through the house, securing everything. Once he had the doors locked and alarm set, he pulled the blackout drapes in the bedroom. There were a lot of times when his investigations had him sleeping on an opposite schedule. He needed the room as dark as possible for those days. Cannon dropped his towel and crawled beneath the covers next to Xan. Xan didn't make a sound. He was already out cold. Cannon closed his eyes, intent on joining him. It didn't take long. The day had been a rollercoaster that completely kicked his ass. He needed a nap.

Xan didn't know how long he slept. In fact, he had no clue about the day or time. He was disoriented in a way he hadn't been in a long time. Yet he was oddly more at peace than he had ever been. After a quick trip to the bathroom, Xan quietly returned to bed. Cannon hadn't budged. Xan was also very good at moving in total silence. It was a top five skill of an assassin.

On his side, he watched Cannon sleep. He had left the light on in the bathroom and the door cracked for just this reason. Xan wanted to see Cannon's face. Cannon had shown him more kindness than he could recall experiencing. Anyone else would have taken him home and left him to deal. Cannon was a good person. Xan had known that from the first time they met. He just always had a Boy Scout personality Xan expected to hate. In some ways, it was annoying. But that trait also made him gentle and caring. Those were equally things Xan expected to make him sick. He had been taught those were undesirable qualities. They made people weak. Xan wanted more. He craved absorbing the sickening sweetness like a sponge.

His body stirred at the memory of how Cannon had gently washed him and cared for his wounds. God. He hadn't known he had a kindness kink. With his arm curled beneath his head, Cannon slept on his side, facing Xan. Xan's gaze moved over him. He was incredibly sexy. Cut body. Gorgeous skin. In his sleep, he looked almost innocent. Cannon rolled to his back and stretched. Xan lost the battle against himself. He didn't pounce. Xan didn't want to startle Cannon. But Xan also didn't give Cannon a chance to wake up enough to deny him. He straddled Cannon's body and claimed his mouth.

Cannon's lips shaped a smile against his. "Good morning," Cannon said, chuckling against his lips.

Xan didn't laugh. He had a mission. His tongue stroked Cannon's as he savored the sensation of Cannon going hard beneath him. They had been dancing around this, whether Cannon realized it or not. Cannon wanted to be something he wasn't. He wanted to bury his desires behind fervor for his job. But the guy's eyes gave him away and Xan intended to set him free.

"I want you." Xan made the admission between kisses, hoping to keep Cannon distracted. "I plan to fuck you."

A sexy whimper escaped Cannon, telling Xan all he needed to know. Cannon wouldn't say no.

"Where's the lube? I need to make you leak with my cum."

Cannon's arm shot out. He patted the table beside the bed until he returned with a cold tube. That was all the permission Xan needed. He quickly coated his fingers. Xan tried distracting Cannon with kisses while testing Cannon's flexibility. He maneuvered his way between Cannon's thighs and dragged the guy's legs over his shoulders. On his knees, with Cannon's legs in the air, Xan wet and stretched Cannon's hole. He met Cannon's stare and didn't look away as he positioned his dick against Cannon's asshole. Xan knew the guy deserved some foreplay, but he also knew Cannon might back down if given too much time to think.

Xan leaned his weight forward, pushing his way inside. Cannon panted for breath as his body gave way, accepting Xan. Xan grabbed the top edge of the headboard for leverage and rolled his abs. His hips moved while he used his core strength against Cannon. He held Cannon's stare. Xan felt his intensity. Cannon never looked away. His expression screamed desire. The way his face flushed, and his eyes took on a dreamy glint, had Xan incapable of seeing anything else. Xan's body never stopped the steady workout. Sweat beaded on his skin as his abs bunched and rolled. They were connected. Cannon stared up at him as if transfixed. Xan couldn't see anything but the neediness etched on Cannon's face.

Cannon whimpered.

The sound had something dark rising inside Xan. "That's it. You're such a good boy, taking it like a champ. I can go all day or come quick. You decide. Let me feel this hole twitch with your pleasure."

Cannon's fingertips lightly skimmed Xan's sides before falling away again, as if he didn't know what to do with his hands. He tried taking what he wanted from Xan's dick, but Xan had him pinned just the way he wanted him. Xan kept him folded like a pretzel as he used his strength to take the pleasure he sought. He knew the angle would make Cannon insane. Cannon gasped for air. Xan never broke pace. He also didn't break eye contact. Xan needed Cannon to see and accept who fucked him. Cannon wasn't dealing with anyone he was used to being with. Xan could be cold, possessive, and deadly. He hadn't been given the same tools to build healthy relationships as most people. Xan had been taught to use every skill he had to manipulate and terminate. He could make this last all day until Cannon begged.

Cannon didn't make it that long. "Please? Oh, God. Please?"

A smile that felt evil as hell pulled at Xan's lips. He changed angles and rhythm. Cannon gasped and scratched at the sheets. Xan was getting one hell of an ab workout and his side burned where he had been stabbed. All he truly felt was Cannon's tight little asshole massaging his cock with each thrust.

Cum shot from Cannon. His body jerked and his asshole convulsed.

A quiet, wicked-sounding chuckle fell from Xan's lips. "You can do better than that." Xan pulled out and flipped Cannon. A tired-sounding whimper escaped Cannon as Xan forced him to his knees. Xan impaled him from behind, taking him hard. Mewling sounds muffled against the mattress. Xan slammed inside Cannon. In no time, the sounds Cannon made turned desperate again.

Xan hummed. He was getting close. "That's right, beautiful. Give me that second orgasm. You have no idea how your ass feels. Fuck. Let me feel that spasm again."

Cannon's cries got louder and more desperate by the second. Sweat rolled down Xan's spine. He worked harder, fucking Cannon like a beast. His body smacked against Cannon's ass with every thrust. Xan's muscles clenched. His balls tightened. Sweat burned his eyes. A cry tore out beneath him. Cannon's body suddenly tried sucking him deeper. It was obvious the second orgasm was stronger than the first. Xan sucked in a sharp breath as he saw stars. His back bowed as he pumped Cannon full of jizz. Every twitch of his dick pulled another moan from his throat. He hadn't blown so hard in ages. His entire body lit like a candle. He couldn't stop pumping inside Cannon, savoring every second of his hot hole.

"Fuck, Cannon. Your asshole is amazing. I don't want to pull out. I'd keep going, but I want you to let me fuck you again." Even as he made the claim, Xan considered taking it back. He had been trained to please. Xan could easily stay hard and ensure Cannon couldn't sit down after this. A hint of sanity returned. He truly wanted Cannon to come back for seconds. That wouldn't happen if he felt abused.

Xan forced himself to pull out. He didn't move away, though. Xan kept Cannon's cheeks spread so he could watch his cum run from Cannon's asshole. Satisfaction purred inside him. They had to be tested regularly as part of their professions.

Their jobs required them to go under-cover. That sometimes meant doing risky things, and more often than not, coming in contact with blood. He wasn't worried about exchanging body fluids. It was currently Xan's job to know everything about Cannon. They were good.

"Fuck. That's sexy. You should see the way my load slips from your sexy asshole and runs to your balls. Goddamn. You make me want to eat it."

"Oh, god."

Xan felt the way his expression turned wicked at Cannon's whispered words. He would twist Cannon around his finger. Cannon thought he understood obsession. He had never known anyone like Xan. Xan would shatter him.

Chapter Six

Fuck. That was all Cannon thought each time he looked at Xan. Just, fuck. That intensity. Wow! That use of body control. Goddamn. Cannon wasn't sure he would ever be the same again. He didn't think he could touch anyone else and not see the way Xan's body had moved while taking him. That experience had been... fuck. It was no wonder Knight would overlook anything for Royal. If Royal had the same intensity, and the guy certainly looked as if he did, then damn. Cannon couldn't blame the guy for looking right through Cannon now. Cannon couldn't compete.

Xan sat across from him, eating the breakfast Cannon made in a borrowed pair of Cannon's workout shorts. Cannon had to force himself to not stare at the guy with stars in his eyes. The problem was, Cannon knew how Xan had ended up so focused and skilled. It hurt his chest, and that one thought led to a thousand more.

"Is Knight in danger? Does he need to worry men like that will come for Royal and him?"

Xan stopped with a bite of eggs halfway to his mouth. His expression changed to unreadable. He set his fork down. "No. Your precious Knight is perfectly safe."

Xan stood and carried his plate to the sink. "I need to figure out a way home."

Cannon scrambled to fix things. "That's not what I meant." He shot to his feet and overcame Xan. His lips automatically touched a deep scar beneath Xan's nape. "I'm trying to understand. That's all. This isn't about Knight. I'm trying to see what you see when it comes to this entire situation. How is Royal safe, but you're not? You said none of you were free. Help me understand."

Xan's muscles relaxed. He turned in Cannon's arms and kissed his forehead. His arms stayed locked around Cannon's waist as he leaned back against the counter. "Royal and I aren't the same. Quentin purchased Royal and then set him free. In the eyes of the society, he belongs to Quentin. He's literally Quentin's property."

"You said Quentin saved you too."

Xan nodded. "He did. I was loaned to a man in the U.S. for a hit job. Afterward, I was supposed to go straight back to Russia and await my next job or for someone to buy me." Xan lifted his arm and showed the back of it to Cannon. There was a small but ragged scar, as if the injury had been deep and hadn't been stitched. "They had me chipped. I dug it out and ran. Along the way, I met this guy who I had known from my days with the Society. He said there was a man who helped people like me start new lives." Xan made a gesture as if searching for a way to explain. "Think of Quentin's place like the Underground Railroad. He takes in not only people he's saved, but people who are running, and people who are brought to him after rescue. If he has room, he'll take them. If he can't, he helps financially. He's a good man," Xan stressed. Cannon was starting to see that. Xan kept going. "Anyhow, I showed up at his door. We spoke, and he gave me a room. He helped me set up a new identity, get therapy, and called in some favors to get me a good job. Quentin is the reason I'm still here. He saved me, but I'm not the same as the guys he's bought. Those people are as free now as people like us can be. The Russian Society was never paid for me. They want that money. The government doesn't negotiate, but they do protect. Most of the time, they see me as untouchable. I guess being alone in the woods with you was too much temptation. There was no way they could know that was a safe house. I'm never far from help. But yeah, that's how Royal is different."

Goddamn it. Xan was right. Knight too. This issue wasn't black and white. Quentin was doing what even the United States government wouldn't, and Cannon had helped shut him down. While Quentin hadn't been and wouldn't be arrested, he couldn't help anyone else. He would have to stay squeaky clean for the rest of his life to avoid another investigation. Quentin was on law enforcement's radar now, and it was partially Cannon's fault. Fuck. Just once, he wanted to be on the side of good.

Cannon kissed Xan's chest. "I can take you home. If you still want to go?"

Xan buried his fingers in Cannon's hair and tugged, forcing Cannon to meet his stare. "That's not what I want, but it's what I have to do." He bit Cannon's bottom lip, weakening his knees. "I have to check in with work."

Cannon fought a whimper. His dick was hard again, but his ass was sore. Truthfully, no one had been inside him in years. He hadn't complained about the lack of preparation, and he wouldn't. Cannon recognized a good thing when it came his way.

He stole a kiss. "Let me find us a couple of shirts and I'll drive you. I'll call Gable along the way and find out where your things are."

Xan grabbed his ass and hauled him forward. Their lower bodies met. Xan was hard for him too. "Just so you know, we're not finished. We both need to deal with work, but this isn't over."

Cannon nodded. His mind might be fuzzy with lust, but he wasn't stupid. This one hundred percent wasn't finished. Cannon was an obsessive bastard and his heart had found its next target.

Sex had definitely changed something between them. Xan went through his day, trying to think about anything else. Except the sweet way they had kissed before Cannon had left him wouldn't purge from his mind. Again, new kindness kink unlocked. After tons of therapy and even some in-patient psychological help, when Xan had finally reached the point where he was even the slightest bit willing to have sex again, he hadn't made love to anyone. He hadn't connected with anyone. The act had been just that: an act. Not with Cannon. Yeah, Xan had fucked him, but something else happened too. He wanted to do it again before he put a label on things.

Gable stuck his head in Xan's office. "Some updates for you."

Xan pulled his mind from its fantasies to focus on the FBI agent who had been assigned to move between his alphabet branch and the CIA to keep Xan informed about every move Cannon made. He was exactly that: a loose cannon. Xan didn't think he had a full grip on him yet.

"What's up?"

"He tried to question the suspects from the warehouse. Jake informed him they'd been scooped up by Homeland."

"So he's back to work, then?"

Gable nodded. "That was my second update. He didn't exactly apologize to Jake, but Jake didn't figure he would."

Despite himself, Xan laughed. "No. He's not the type."

A hint of worry pinched Gable's features. His dark green gaze slid away.

Xan nearly groaned. "What else?"

Gable winced. "He's just arrived at Royal's place."

Xan ground his back teeth so hard his jaw popped. "I see. Do we still have audio?"

Gable nodded. "That's why I rushed to get you."

Xan pushed to his feet and circled his desk. He tried not to look as pissed off as he was, but the way the dark-haired agent scrambled out of his way said he must not have done a good job. Xan made his way to the surveillance room.

"Cut the recording. Everyone out."

Buttons were flipped, and people scattered. Once he was alone, Xan grabbed the closest set of headphones. He got there just in time to see Cannon waiting on Knight and Royal's porch. His eye twitched. Apparently, today, it wasn't even good enough for Cannon to silently stalk. Cannon had to see Knight. The rage was thick. He couldn't believe Cannon could kiss him the way he had and then run to Knight. The audacity was un-believable.

Knight's front door opened with the force of anger Xan would expect at Cannon's unwelcome appearance.

Knight stood in the doorway. He looked as enraged as Xan felt. When he spoke, he sounded tired. "What now?"

Cannon held up his hands, as if showing his surrender. "It's nothing like you think. Is Royal home too? I'd like to talk to you both."

Royal appeared at Knight's side, as if he had lingered just out of sight in case he was needed.

Cannon nodded. "Good. I'd like to get this out in one spiel." He took an audible breath. "I'm sorry for any way I might have upset either of you. Things in my life have been a bit of a mess for a long time, but that's neither here nor there, I guess. I'm happy for you." He focused on Knight. "I truly am happy for you. We used to be friends, and I never meant to do anything to hurt you. I know you love Royal." To Xan's shock, Cannon focused on Royal. "And I know you deserve to be loved by someone as amazing as Knight. You don't have to worry about seeing me again. Obviously, I know you were never really worried about me, but you get what I mean. I've lost my friend, and that's my fault. I hope you two have an amazing life together."

Xan's spine collapsed against the chair. He didn't know what to think. For sure, he hadn't expected this, though.

Cannon obviously didn't intend to stick around to see how his apology was received. He turned and jogged down the porch steps. Xan watched Knight and Royal exchange a glance. Royal gave a small nod and Knight went after him. They moved from camera range and Xan couldn't hear what was said or see what happened. But Royal moved to the steps and sat, watching. Xan knew nothing would happen under Royal's supervision. For a moment, Xan stared at nothing in shock. Why had Cannon done this?

Xan stood. He had to see Cannon again. Unfortunately, he couldn't ask about the visit without tipping his hand too far. But still, Xan had to see him. He opened the door and found Gable waiting.

Xan met his gaze. "Keep the cameras two more weeks. If Cannon doesn't turn up again, I think we're safe to pull surveillance."

Gable dipped his chin, acknowledging the order. Things felt like they were finally settling down for Royal and Knight. Xan had a feeling things were just getting started for him.

Chapter Seven

Cannon hadn't truly known where to start with getting his life together. He only knew he had to get some shit straight. There was no future in him wallowing in self-pity or drinking himself into an early grave. Maybe he had needed that time on ice. Possibly he needed to remember he had done good things during his time with the FBI. He had stopped bad guys from doing worse things. Mostly, Cannon simply recognized he had been wrong about some things.

As much as Cannon had known in his heart Knight had never deserved the hell Cannon had put him through, there had been a small part of him that brushed that knowledge aside. After all, Knight took him back time and time again. When Knight had met Royal, and found real love, it had been easier to blame Royal than himself. That wasn't the case, though. If Royal showed Knight half the intensity Xan had shown him, it was no wonder Knight would do anything to keep him. Even if that meant marrying a contract killer for the CIA. Unfortunately, that line of thought circled all the way around to him, believing what was easy. Xan was right. A lot of these people they killed were better off dead. While

Quentin's money had proven that was all it took to make charges disappear, that was exactly why it had enraged Cannon. Quentin might be a good man, but he was one in a million. Too many times, it wasn't the good guys using their influence. That didn't mean Jake was on the take with every single one. Jake didn't run the entire country. But if there were people out there like Royal, taking these people out before they could use their influence to do whatever they wanted, well then, who was Cannon to argue?

That meant Cannon owed some apologies. It had been hard as hell, swallowing his pride. He hoped he didn't have to do it again. It wasn't like he had forgotten Royal got him fired, but then again, maybe he'd gotten himself fired. Cannon didn't know which way was up any longer. Seeing beneath Xan's hard shell had truly fucked with him. He felt like he didn't know himself anymore.

Cannon thought he would do his research on the drug house and try to get back on track. His mind wouldn't cooperate. He couldn't stop thinking about the way Xan had held his stare as he fucked him. Holy hell. It had been the hottest moment of his entire life, and that was saying a lot. Knight was pretty damn smoking in bed. There had been a reason he couldn't stay away.

Thankfully, his doorbell rang, pulling him from his thoughts and the forgotten surveillance video. He checked the peephole. Xan stood on the other side. He was in a suit and was back to looking like the cold agent Cannon had dealt with since crossing Quentin. Cannon prepared himself to get his feelings hurt when Xan pretended they hadn't slept together. He took a deep breath and opened the door.

"Hey."

Xan didn't respond. He stepped inside, forcing Cannon to take a step back. Xan kicked the door closed behind him as he overcame Cannon and claimed his mouth. Immediately, Cannon couldn't breathe. He was kindling, and Xan tossed a lit match. Cannon burned. But more than that, a feeling in his chest stirred. He felt alive, like he hadn't in years.

"I got to work and couldn't stop thinking about you." Cannon's heart soared at the confession. Xan kept going. "I needed to come back and find out why."

Cannon ran his hands up Xan's chest. "Have you figured it out?"

Xan shook his head. "Not yet."

"Then you'd better keep trying." Cannon reclaimed Xan's mouth.

The room spun. Cannon's back hit the door. Buttons went flying as Xan ripped open his shirt. Cannon fought through gasps as Xan kissed a path down Cannon's body, biting and licking. All Cannon could do was watch as Xan dropped to his knees. If anyone had ever acted so desperately to have him, Cannon couldn't recall it. Then his dick was in Xan's mouth, and it took all Cannon's strength to stay upright.

"Fuck." Cannon dragged out the word as his head hit the door.

Xan had no mercy in his heart. He scrambled Cannon's brains. Cannon was ready to do whatever Xan asked. Xan sucked and bobbed. He swallowed. Cannon switched between trying to watch and fighting the pleasure to keep his eyes open. Dirty images flew through Cannon's head. He wanted to do everything with this man. Cannon knew in his heart Xan would do everything with zero reserve. God, he couldn't wait to find out.

Sounds came from the back of his throat. He ran his fingers through Xan's hair, fighting the urge to use Xan. His breathing turned ragged as he neared the edge. Cannon's skin tightened. His toes curled. Xan shot to his feet and claimed his mouth, swallowing Cannon's cries as he finished him off with his hand. Cannon wasn't disappointed. It was Xan. They were together. He had never been happier, and that fucked with him hard. Xan had seemingly come from nowhere to take over his every thought. The guy had gone from threatening Cannon's life and job to becoming the reason Cannon wanted to keep breathing. It was scary as hell. He didn't want to stop.

Goddamn. Cannon was every bit as responsive as Xan remembered. He had begun to wonder if he had simply made their encounter bigger in his mind. No. His memory wasn't big enough. Xan was fascinated. People didn't hold his interest. Mostly because he rarely trusted anyone, especially anyone who didn't come from his same background. It didn't make sense for it to be Cannon who caught him. They couldn't be more different. Outside of the jobs they held, they had nothing. Well, they both enjoyed a daily workout. Their time together at the cabin had been peaceful. The sex was off the charts and they both liked the same TV shows and music. Damn it. They had shit in common. He fucking wanted this.

Xan couldn't stop kissing him. "I've never wanted to watch someone come again so badly in my life," he admitted between kisses.

He felt Cannon smile against his lips. His stomach nearly growled from the hunger that one gesture caused. Cannon's hands found Xan's belt.

Xan stopped him. He wiped the cum on his hand on the tail of Cannon's ruined shirt. "Not yet. I only want to come inside you and I know you're still sore."

Cannon's expression had Xan fighting a moan. He looked exactly like a man who had just been well loved. "I don't want you suffering."

A smile exploded across Xan's face. He genuinely liked Cannon. "I can take it."

Cannon licked his lips. "But you don't have to. If you need to be inside me, I'm willing."

Xan went flush against Cannon. "Baby, I want you more than willing. I don't want to take it easy so I can maybe have you later. When I take you, I need you completely ready. I plan to fuck you hard." His gaze dropped to Cannon's mouth. He couldn't resist stealing another nibble of Cannon's plump bottom lip. Need clawed at his insides, but he wasn't weak. Still, he knew Cannon didn't understand. In this way, they were as different as two people could be.

He chose to explain. "Orgasm denial was a big part of our training." Xan watched Cannon's expression snap closed, but he kept going. If they planned to do this, Cannon needed to understand him. "Men tend to think too much with their dicks. They needed to break us from that. Some people were very literally broken. Needless to say, I don't consider waiting for you as suffering, especially because I'm choosing to be patient." Xan swiped his lips across Cannon's. "You deserve better than to be used. Even when I'm rough with you, never doubt you're being cherished."

Cannon was the one who came for the kiss this time. He sucked Xan's bottom lip before curling his tongue upward, as if trying to lick the roof of Xan's mouth. Xan's knees weakened. He had to force himself to stay upright. Cannon kissed like a man who loved to use his mouth and had expert-level training. He tested Xan's will. Xan had to find something else to do before he made a liar of himself. At the moment, he felt weak. He took a step back. "Let's get cleaned up. I'll take you to dinner."

A sexy smile lit Cannon's features. "I'd love that." His gaze slid past Xan. Cannon's features changed, turning confused. "Holy shit." He fixed his clothes and headed toward a monitor on his coffee table. It was obvious he had set up a surveillance center in his living room.

"Is that who I think it is?" He pointed at a man on the screen.

Xan moved to stand at his side. An ex-police captain who had been forced into retirement due to suspicion of illegal activity stood in the driveway of the drug house. He looked around, as if watching to make sure no one saw him. Cannon snatched up his phone and quickly scrolled before pressing the device to his ear. In the otherwise silent room, Xan heard the ringing on the other end.

"Hamilton."

"I know who the supplier is."

Xan stared at Cannon while he broke down the clues that had finally snapped together in his mind. They painted the full image of a station on the take, finally solving months of missing seized drugs and evidence disappearing. Pride grew in Xan's chest. Cannon had just solved something the DEA had been working on forever and couldn't crack. Cannon had been put on the case only because deaths from the drugs traced back to that house had started crossing state lines. Even in his resentment toward the FBI, he couldn't stop his amazing mind. Xan was in trouble. He wanted to keep him.

CHAPTER EIGHT

AFTER ACCEPTING HIS FIFTH congratulation from a coworker, Cannon had to admit he would be lying if he said he wasn't proud. He needed the win. Saving Xan had been personal. Cannon had truly needed this reminder he was good at what he did. He had gotten this job and climbed through the ranks for a reason. Everything still required paperwork, unfortunately. At least he didn't have to squint at the computer monitor today.

The phone rang on his desk. Cannon bit back a sigh. Fortunately, he knew what to expect this time when he picked up the receiver.

"Whitley."

"You know the drill."

Cannon pinched the spot between his eyes. "On my way."

Cannon stood and headed for Jake's office. There was still a part of him that didn't care if he lost this job. He had no idea what he would do next. But he had a pretty fucking spotless record, so he would figure it out. This time, he knocked.

"Come in."

Cannon stepped inside Jake's office. For the first time, Cannon realized how ridiculously clean the place was. There wasn't a thing out of place. There also wasn't a single thing personal about it. Not a picture or even a plant. Just a spotless void of unhappiness.

"You wanted to see me."

Jake held out a stack of files. "Your next case."

With a dip of his chin, Cannon crossed the room and took the files. He would look at them later. After he finished his reports. Jake said nothing else. Cannon hesitated. His pride twinged, but if he planned to stay, then they needed to bury the hatchet.

"For what it's worth, I'm sorry for our disagreement." There. He wasn't sorry for what he said, but he regretted they had argued. They still had to work together.

Jake leaned back in his chair and eyed Cannon. He blew out a sigh. "For what's it's worth, I regret sending you to the cabin. I hope one day you can understand my job sometimes requires choosing the greater good. It's not always an easy decision to overlook one thing to stop a worse thing, you understand?"

Cannon gave him a sharp nod. He got it.

Jake held his stare, looking more intense than Cannon had ever seen him. "I also want you to understand the only person who pays me to make these decisions is Uncle Sam, and it's nowhere near enough most days."

Cannon gave another nod, even though he wasn't sure he believed it. The anger and obvious feeling of being insulted was in Jake's eyes and voice, though. If

Cannon had the guy in interrogation, he would say the man told the truth.

Jake dipped his chin. "Get back to work, then."

Cannon headed back to his desk, feeling slightly defeated. It seemed like he had lost a lot of rounds lately. He was apologizing right and left, even when he still wasn't sure he was wrong. Sometimes Cannon wanted to walk away from everything. Start a new life. Become someone new. He hadn't lived any sort of life in years. Work had dominated every second. He actually had a pretty fat savings. Every now and then, he thought about buying his own cabin in the woods and going off grid for a while. Those weeks alone in the woods with Xan hadn't made him any less exhausted. He needed that full time. Two weeks was nowhere near enough. Truthfully, he was burned out with the entire grind. Maybe it was time to quit. He had lost his love for this.

Cannon stared at his computer screen. His gaze moved between the screen and his case files. Did he really want to start a new case? His phone buzzed on his desk. Cannon grabbed it. A smile exploded across his face at the sight of Xan's name.

Xan: *Are you finished being sore yet?*

A loud snort escaped Cannon. He covered his nose and mouth at the sound. There was no squashing his smile.

Cannon: *I told you last night you could have me then. But yes, I'm fine.*

"Is that smile for me?"

Cannon nearly jumped out of his skin when Xan appeared at his cubicle. "Holy shit." He patted his chest, trying to calm the rapid beating of his heart.

Xan's sexy smile didn't show a hint of remorse. "I came to steal you away for lunch."

God, he was beautiful. Cannon was getting too attached. "Sounds great." He opened his desk drawer and tossed the case files inside before locking the drawer. "I'm not getting anywhere on these reports anyway."

Cannon shifted to his feet. They were inches apart. The temptation to kiss Xan was crippling. A massive realization struck. Cannon wanted to keep him, and he didn't care who knew.

The lack of patience to see Cannon again was getting a little scary. Xan hadn't even made it through the day. The thing was, though, Xan wasn't accustomed to having feelings for someone. He didn't know how to regulate. Xan kept needing to go to Cannon and see if the last time had been a fluke. Each time, he couldn't stop smiling. Couldn't stop craving. He was in trouble, and he didn't know how to stop acting desperate for Cannon. Xan also didn't think he wanted to quit.

Despite his best efforts to play it cool at Cannon's work, he couldn't stop casting Cannon heated looks on the way to the parking garage. He had intentionally parked in a corner where no one could see inside. The moment they were inside and out of sight, Xan overcame Cannon. Cannon didn't scoff. They went hard at each other, as if they hadn't seen each other in weeks.

"Mhmm. Best lunch I've ever had," Cannon said between kisses. Laughter filled his voice.

Xan pulled away. "Just in case you think I don't intend to feed you." He grabbed a bag from the backseat. "An Italian sub on wheat."

A happy-sounding laugh burst from Cannon. "Thanks. I can eat that at my desk later." He snagged Xan's tie and hauled him in for another kiss.

There was so much happiness and hope in Xan's chest. It had nowhere to go, so Xan poured it into Cannon. They made out, kissing and touching. Their fingers kept linking. Xan had never felt this way. He didn't fully understand what he felt. All Xan knew was he didn't want it to stop.

"Tell me you're mine and only mine."

Cannon's demand made Xan realize he wasn't alone. This had turned into something along the way. It was more than sexual attraction.

Xan's gaze moved over Cannon's face. Their fingers still played. "Is that what you want?"

Cannon smiled. It was sexy and wicked. "I don't know what's happening between us, but I know I want it to keep happening." His smile fell and picked up again, as if Cannon had a hard time holding on to it. "I also know I don't want to share you."

Xan didn't take the conversation lightly. "That's fair, since I fear for you if I found you with anyone else."

Cannon's expression made the confession worthwhile. It was like Xan had said he loved him. Cannon's gaze dropped to Xan's mouth. "We'll finish this at my place later. Pack a bag." Then Cannon was right back in Xan's space, gnawing his bottom lip and curling his tongue around Xan's. Something had definitely changed between them. Xan wanted even more.

Cannon moved back to his seat. Turned sideways with his head leaned against the seat, he held Xan's stare. "Do you ever think about walking away from everything and starting a new life?"

The question caught Xan off guard. He gave it some real consideration. Xan had enjoyed those weeks of peace at the cabin with Cannon. Still, he couldn't see himself in any other life. "No."

Cannon's gaze slid away. He looked defeated. "Oh."

Xan tried to explain. "My career wasn't earned the typical way. The fact that I can run an entire team for the CIA, that was unimaginable for me at one point in my life." Xan made a helpless gesture. He didn't know how to explain what Cannon could never understand. "You're special. You have all the options in the universe to be whatever you want to be. All I know how to do is this, and I owe it to people like me to not give up."

Cannon stared at him, as if he saw his soul. He didn't respond. Cannon had him a little worried.

"Should I be concerned?"

A wry smile touched Cannon's lips. He shook his head. "It was just a question."

Xan had a bad feeling in his gut. He felt something and Xan didn't want to lose that. Unfortunately, as good as he was at his job, he wasn't good at close relationships. He could charm people or kill them. Xan didn't know how to love them or be supportive. Cannon needed something Xan didn't know how to provide, so he kissed him and hoped it was enough.

Chapter Nine

Xan: *How's the new case going?*

Cannon: *Fine. It's in that boring stage. You know how it goes.*

Xan: *Jake tells me you're at the coroner. You're the only person I know who finds that boring.*

Cannon: *I've been here a million times. It's just dead people who went badly. Another day of me trying to figure it out.*

Xan: *You sound tired. Is that my fault?*

Cannon. *That's the best kind of tired.*

Xan: *Do you want me to do it again?*

Cannon: *Absolutely.*

Cannon: *I'm nearby. Want to meet for lunch?*

Xan: *I'm in. Just let me know where.*

Cannon: *Coming over tonight?*

Xan: *Don't I always?*

Cannon: *Just checking.*

Xan: *Sounds like someone misses me.*

Cannon: *Always.*

Four months with Xan and going strong. Some days, Cannon couldn't believe it. He hadn't expected to last this long with anyone, especially Xan. Damn, he was so thankful, though. He had never been happier. Xan didn't hide him. Cannon didn't either. Unlike everyone else Cannon had ever dated, Xan hadn't once brought up meeting his parents. He didn't expect a big coming-out speech. They were just a couple. A happy couple. No pressure, just a love Cannon couldn't stop from growing bigger every day. The thing about that was, it meant the strain came from within. Each day, Cannon craved a little more. He wanted everyone to have no doubts about their status. Cannon hated that Xan hadn't gone with him to celebrate his birthday with his parents. Every day, everything Cannon did without Xan felt a little hollower. Cannon had a bad feeling he had finally met the one, and he didn't think Xan truly felt the same way. No demands usually meant no deep feelings. Cannon honestly believed Xan still thought of them as casually dating. Neither of them wanted to see anyone else, but obviously, Xan would be fine if he woke up tomorrow and never saw Cannon again. It stung.

That didn't stop Cannon from trying to coax Xan out of his clothes. Xan was being extra teasing today. While straddling Xan's lap, Cannon sucked Xan's neck. He loved the sounds Xan made. When the knocks started, Cannon thought it was his heart pounding in his ears. Then the doorbell rang several times.

Cannon looked toward the door, and Xan and Cannon exchanged glances. Cannon snagged his phone and checked his front door camera. His heart tried climbing into his throat. "It's my parents." He stood, unsure of what to do. Cannon didn't want to tell Xan to hide, but he also hadn't considered what he would say if they ever came face to face with his parents as a couple.

Xan pushed to his feet. He handed Cannon his shirt. "I'll go wait in bed. Join me when you can." He didn't look hurt or disappointed. Cannon was, though. He was on both points. Possibly a part of him wanted to be left with no choice.

When Xan disappeared down the hall, Cannon pulled on his shirt and made sure it hid his erection. He ran his hand over his head, trying to flatten his hair. Cannon took a deep breath and opened the door.

He ran his hand over his hair again. "Sorry. I was sleeping. How long have you two been knocking?"

Neither one smiled. They were also together in the middle of the day on a Tuesday. His mom answered. "Not long. We saw your car. Why are you home in the middle of the week? Are you sick?"

Cannon took a step back, inviting them inside. "You know my schedule is a mess. I might go a month with no time off and then be off a week. It's always been that way."

They moved to the couch and sat.

Cannon quickly closed his laptop on the coffee table before they saw anything they didn't have clearance to see.

His dad's dark brown gaze moved over his face. "Did we catch you watching porn?"

Cannon rolled his eyes without thinking. "I'm working surveillance. You know I can't let anyone see classified information."

His dad gave him a sharp nod, as if satisfied his son hadn't been sinning. Cannon's irritation unexpectedly grew. He had been so close to letting them meet Xan. Now he was back to feeling like a kid called to the carpet about a decision that should completely be his at thirty-four goddamn years old.

His parents exchanged glances as if having a silent conversation. Cannon's anxiety grew. He needed a minute between being on the edge of getting fucked and lectured.

"Do you want something to drink?"

His mom shook her head and patted the spot next to her on the couch. The dread got worse. When he sat, she dug inside her purse and brought out a cream-colored envelope. She held it out to Cannon.

Cannon's eyebrows rose, but he accepted and opened the card. It was an invitation. His heart beat a little faster and his pulse sounded louder in his ears. It was an invite to Knight and Royal's wedding. The date was for the previous weekend. Cannon lifted his chin. He didn't know what to say.

It seemed his mom did. "At first, we hoped Royal was just an odd name for a girl. It wasn't until we attended that a lot of reality hit, and questions were answered. You don't look surprised."

Cannon handed back the invitation. "I'm only surprised you went."

She stuffed the envelope back in his purse. "Why wouldn't we go? Knight's been like a part of the family for years. Of course we went."

Cannon nodded. His gaze slid between his parents. He didn't know what to say.

His dad cleared his throat. "You weren't there."

"I wasn't invited."

The couple exchanged another glance. Cannon thought the tension might snap his brain. His tongue got away from him. "What? Ask what you came to ask."

His mom took his hand. Cannon wanted to snatch it back. "Knight and you were so close for so many years. Sometimes we wondered…"

His dad picked up where his mom trailed off. "When we didn't see you at the wedding, it kind of made us realize that maybe Knight and you were a bit more than friends." As if he worried he might insult the fuck out of Cannon, he rushed to say the rest. "I mean, you two were inseparable for a while and then you wouldn't know anything about his life. Then you would be inseparable again. You're not married yet and you haven't brought anyone home for us to meet."

His mom cut in. "You never talk about anything relationship-wise at all and that's just not normal for someone your age. I know you say work is always busy, but I know it's never *that* busy."

Cannon's gaze moved between them. They looked like they equally held their breath. There would never be another chance like this. If he lied, it would twice as hard to take it back. Still, he couldn't say the words without being a hundred percent certain it was what he wanted. He also needed to buy his indecision a few more seconds. "Are you asking if I'm gay too?" Cannon needed the clarification before he leveled his life.

This time, they didn't look at each other to ensure they were on the same page. They nodded.

Cannon tried taking a breath. He hoped he didn't puke. They stared at him so intently. Cannon didn't want to lose them. They would never feel the same about him after this.

Xan strolled into the room wearing a tank top and workout shorts. He was barefoot and looked as if he lived there. His smile was pure charm. He looked like a man anyone would be proud to know.

"I thought I heard voices."

His parents looked between Xan and Cannon and back again. Cannon nearly laughed at their shock. He tossed Xan a grateful look. It seemed the decision was out of his hands.

Cannon motioned toward Xan. "Mom. Dad. This is Xan Akim. Xan, Wyatt and Maria Whitley."

Xan shook hands with the pair and then claimed the recliner. "I wondered when I would get to meet you two."

Wyatt's eyebrows rose. He looked Cannon's way. "A Russian?"

The desire to laugh doubled. Nothing about being gay. Just Russian. Maybe his dad still didn't understand. A bright smile lit Cannon's face without his permission. "*Special Agent* Xan Akim with the CIA. Also, my boyfriend."

To his shock, both his parents beamed. His mom spoke on both their behalf. "It's nice to *finally* meet you. We were getting pretty tired of being in the dark."

A kind smile touched Xan's lips. "In Cannon's defense, we both have insane case-work schedules."

His mom turned her wrath on him. She smacked his arm. "Now tell me about Knight." She shot a quick glance Xan's way. "As long as that doesn't make you uncomfortable, of course."

Xan made a dismissive gesture. "They've been friends a long time. Can I get either of you something to drink?"

"Coffee would be kind of nice," his dad muttered, as if unsure if he should ask.

Xan stood. "Coffee coming up."

Cannon waited until Xan disappeared into the kitchen before focusing on his mom. He didn't really know where to start, so he just picked a place. "Um, so, I guess you could say Knight and I have been off and on over the years, but always stayed good friends. Obviously, he loves you both. When he started dating Royal, I had some reservations. The guy has a bit of a shady past, but they love each other, and I should've stayed out of it. Long story short, we had a falling out over it. We've somewhat made up since then. But it'll be a long time, if ever, before I get any invitations to anything in his life."

His mom went on a short rant in Spanish about him ruining a good friendship. She was hot-tempered like that. Cannon waited her out. Finally, she patted his arm. "With that said." Her gaze moved toward the kitchen and then back to hold his stare. "He is very handsome, and a special agent."

"And with the CIA," his dad chimed in.

Cannon chuckled. "You know the CIA isn't any more powerful than the FBI, right? Plus, I'm also a special agent."

His dad shot him a wry look. "I'm not dumb, son. But—at the end of the day—you're answerable to congress. He's not. His teams can basically do anything as long as no one finds out about it."

He had no idea.

"Not even then, really," Xan said, appearing in the doorway with two cups of coffee. "I didn't know how you two take yours, so I just brought them black. I can grab you whatever you need to doctor your cups."

Both shook their heads.

"Black is fine for us," his dad said. He stayed intently focused on Xan. "What happens if you get caught?" It was beyond obvious Xan had his dad hooked. No one loved conspiracy theories and clandestine missions more than Wyatt Whitley.

Xan reclaimed his seat. "From my experience, everyone collectively decides to look away."

"Did the CIA have Kennedy assassinated?"

Cannon had to look away to keep from laughing at his mom's question.

"Meh. Probably."

At Xan's answer, his dad slapped his knee. "I knew it."

Xan met Cannon's stare. They smiled. Something passed between them. This was love. Full-blown. No going back. Nothing standing between them now. It was love.

Xan would be lying if he claimed he hadn't immediately stopped outside the living room to eavesdrop before Cannon let his parents inside. One thing Xan was a master at was reading people. Cannon saw his parents through the lens of a child. Xan listened to the underlying cadence of their voices. They loved their son. The pair just wanted to be let in. As much as Xan didn't truly want to meet the parents, he couldn't let Cannon drown. Left on his own, he might have denied being gay, and then his life would have gone down the toilet. The guilt and hiding would continue to eat away at his sanity until he destroyed everything they were building together. So, Xan had taken the choice from his hands. It had been a gamble, but Xan put all his chips on love. Cannon loved him. Xan didn't doubt that for a moment.

It felt like it took forever for the pair to leave. After several hugs and promises to visit, they were finally alone. The moment the door closed behind the pair, Cannon's gaze slid his way. Xan did his best to look like a guilty child, even though he didn't have an ounce of re-morse.

Cannon shook his head. "I thought you said you didn't want to meet them."

Xan shrugged. He decided to be honest. "I couldn't let you lose the battle against yourself. You were half a second away from denying the truth and we both know how that would've ended."

"Thank you."

Xan wrapped his arms around Cannon and squeezed. "It went well, I think. Be-sides me being Russian, of course."

Cannon laughed against the crook of his neck, muffling the sound. "Lord, who knows with those two?" Cannon took a ragged-sounding breath against Xan's neck.

Xan's eyes fell closed. He had never felt so much for another person. Cannon's stress and worries were his stress and worries. Xan rubbed his back. "You did great. It's obvious your parents love you more than they love their prejudices. That's a good thing."

"I know. I'm just... I don't know."

Xan kissed his cheek. He got it. Years of fear and hiding were gone, but now there was nothing stopping a future fallout. Maybe his parents' shock would wear off and they wouldn't be as okay as they thought. He practically felt the way Cannon's insides shook. Maybe Xan wasn't who he needed right then.

"Would you like to call Knight and talk about it?"

Cannon's grip on his shirt tightened. "No, but that's sweet. Thank you for that."

Xan held Cannon tighter. "Of course. I love you. There's nothing I wouldn't do for you."

Cannon's head shot up so fast, he nearly knocked out Xan's teeth. "What did you just say?"

Confusion off-balanced Xan. "That I love you. We've been together for months. That wasn't obvious by now?"

A smile exploded across Cannon's face. He laughed. "Everything is so easy with you. It feels complicated."

"I don't know what that means."

Cannon laughed again. "It means I love you too."

"Oh. I knew that."

Cannon shook his head. It was obvious he didn't know how to handle Xan today.

Xan motioned toward the hallway. "I believe we were interrupted."

Cannon paused for a moment. A hint of wickedness touched his features. "Race you." Before Cannon's words had time to fully absorb, Cannon was already on the move. Xan took off after him and overcame him outside the bedroom. He snatched Cannon off his feet and headed for bed. After tossing him on top, Xan followed him down, covering Cannon's body with his. He had never been this happy in his life. Sometimes it hit him at the strangest times how far they had come. Xan had gone from thinking he would have to make Cannon disappear to knowing he couldn't live without the guy. He would give up everything to keep this. Xan understood Royal's insanity when it came to Knight now. He was crazy over Cannon. Xan couldn't get enough.

Cannon laughed at the way Xan tore at his clothes, stripping him as quickly as possible. His impatience was on full display. The laughter died when their nude bodies met. Xan went from not being able to get inside Cannon quickly enough to wanting this to last forever. He took his time lubing Cannon, savoring the way Cannon gasped for air. When he finally slipped inside Cannon, Xan moved slowly, making love to Cannon. They held each other's stare. Xan had never truly connected with anyone the way he had with Cannon. He had already refused to allow his past to rule him, but Xan had thought his emotions were beyond full repair. He had regained his feelings, but they had been muted—like trying to hear through cotton balls. Then Cannon had challenged him, frustrating him while still leaving him aroused. Cannon had shown a fire Xan hadn't known how to douse. Until Xan realized he didn't want to dim Cannon's flame. He wanted to be consumed by it. Everything inside him had exploded into the brightest of colors and sound with Cannon. He didn't know how to mute his emotions when they were together. The way he felt was too powerful. It was more than lust. Xan had finally found one place in the world he never wanted to leave. His chest felt empty when Cannon wasn't around.

Cannon strained against him. He visibly fought his way toward the edge. Xan never looked away. He pumped inside Cannon, holding a slow, steady pace. When Cannon blew, Xan studied every nuance.

"I love you." The desperate-sounding words beneath him broke Xan. He changed angles and took the pleasure he wanted. Cannon whimpered, adding vocals to Xan's lust.

Xan's body tensed. He pressed his forehead against Cannon's and held Cannon's stare. Xan never looked away, even as an orgasm tried taking him out.

"I love you," Xan whispered, giving the words back to Cannon. They were one. He truly understood that saying now. Xan would stalk him to the ends of the earth. He would never let them be apart.

CHAPTER TEN

THE CURSOR BLINKED ON the screen. Cannon truly felt like all he did was paperwork anymore. He hadn't tried talking to Xan about it again, but fuck. Cannon still honestly thought he was done. Surely there was some private sector job for him or something. Even Jake had decided to retire and God only knew who Cannon would be forced to deal with next. It felt like there was something just out of sight, screaming for him to move toward it, and it wasn't here.

For the hundredth time, Cannon pulled up his already written resignation letter and stared at it. He was terrified to pull the trigger. Cannon would miss the occasional adrenaline rush, right? Surely, he couldn't be a bank manager or data entry clerk. He shuddered at the thought. That was why he hadn't hit send. Cannon didn't want to do this anymore, but he also had no clue what he wanted.

"Apparently, there's cake and stuff in the break room."

Cannon quickly minimized his screen and glanced up. "What?"

"For Jake's retirement," Gable expounded. "Cake and whatnot. Want to go?"

Cannon pushed his chair away from the desk. At least it was something to break up the monotony. He fell into step beside Gable on the way to the break room. "I thought you were some sort of liaison between the CIA and us now. Don't you spend most of your time there? I haven't seen you much."

Gable shrugged. "I bounce around a bit. Honestly, I've been hanging around, hoping to hear who they plan to have take Jake's place. Maybe I'll need to put in to stay with the CIA full time, you know?"

Cannon fought the urge to admit he had his resignation letter drawn up already. "Yeah, I feel ya. God forbid we have to report to Dave or some shit."

They both looked Dave's way as they passed. The rat-looking guy had a notebook in his hand, not even bothering to hide the way he took notes on what everyone did. He was the office snitch. Everyone hated him.

Gable looked his way. His green eyes swam with laughter. "Fuck that."

Cannon chuckled. "My thoughts exactly."

Inside the break room, they found a huge cake already half gone and several two-liter bottles of various sodas. Cannon grabbed a red Solo cup for Gable and him.

Gable nodded toward the cake. "I'll grab us a slice. You know what I like to drink."

He did. They had once been partners for years. Cannon knew an unfortunate amount about Gable. That came with too many late nights and stakeouts. Sometimes people said too much when they got tired. Work friends usually knew more about each other than spouses. Surviving hell together and all that.

Gable reappeared with two slices of cake. They traded. One drink for one plate. They stood awkwardly in the corner and ate while people came and went in waves, grabbing their plates before returning to their desks. Gable no longer had a permanent desk here, and Cannon thought he might die if he had to go sit behind his computer again. Neither of them moved.

A new wave of people poured in. Cannon caught a glimpse of a guy's profile. He spent a moment staring, racking his brain as he tried to decide where they had met before. Then the guy next to him turned and their gazes locked. It hit Cannon. His gaze moved between the first guy and his group of friends. It was them. There could be no doubt. They quickly scrambled from the room while Cannon stood in shock.

When he came back to himself, his gaze slid Gable's way. The way Gable stood frozen—like a deer in headlights—he knew he was caught. Cannon calmly set his drink and plate aside. He headed back to his desk.

"Cannon. Wait up. Let me explain."

Cannon didn't look his way. He paused long enough to hit send on his resignation letter and log out. Cannon grabbed his jacket from the back of his chair and headed out with Gable hot on his heels.

"You have to see this from the bureau's point of view."

Cannon didn't stop. He jumped behind the wheel of his car. There was nothing to say. He had been set up and lied to. Tricked so he would fall in line. Most of all, Cannon had fallen in love with a guy who had pretended to get kidnapped and stabbed. Everything in his life was a lie. There was no going back.

"Oh, fuck. Oh, fuck. Fuck. Fuck. Fuck." Gable raced to his nearby car. The CIA and FBI headquarters were both located downtown and were close enough to feasibly walk. That was what Gable chose most days, mostly so he could kill some time outdoors. Thankfully, he drove today. He couldn't get to Xan fast enough. Never in a million years had Gable thought Cannon would cross paths with the team he had put together to kidnap Xan.

"Fuck me!" Gable slapped the steering wheel when he caught a red light. He didn't know if Cannon was headed to kill Xan or what. Gable would never make it there first, but he had a terrible feeling, whatever Cannon had planned, it would be worse than a confrontation.

Gable raced so fast through every checkpoint at CIA headquarters, it took three swipes of his badge each time to unlock each door. He ran the length of the hallway to Xan's office, forcing more than one person to scramble out of his way. When he reached his destination, Gable didn't knock. He ripped the door open like he planned to tear it from its hinges. He was panting by the time he stopped.

Xan sat behind his desk with another man sitting across from him. The guy wore a leather jacket and jeans with biker boots. Gable gave him only a cursory glance before focusing on Xan. He didn't have time to ask for privacy.

"He knows."

Xan didn't react immediately. It was as if he had to search his mind to decide what Gable meant, but there was only one "he" they had in common who was this important.

Xan shot to his feet. "How? You swore to me the team you put together would never cross Cannon's path."

Gable made a helpless gesture. "How was I supposed to know Jake would retire? Free cake always brings the rats from the basement."

The mystery man chuckled.

Xan and Gable shot him death looks.

He cleared his throat and visibly tried going back to pretending he wasn't listening.

Gable focused on Xan. "He immediately jumped into his car and left. I tried to stop him. Then I raced here, thinking he might be headed this way."

Xan scrubbed his forehead. "Fuck! I have to go. Take care of this," he said, motioning toward the man in his office. Gable nodded, even though he had no idea what he was meant to do. Xan raced from the office without looking back. Gable watched him go.

The guy cleared his throat again, reminding Gable of his presence. "I believe I'm the 'this' you're supposed to be taking care of."

Gable's gaze slid the man's way. He had eerie-looking gray eyes. "Do you have any idea what I'm supposed to be doing with you?" He hoped at least one of them wasn't clueless.

A wicked-looking smile stretched the man's lips. Gable held his breath. Suddenly, he couldn't wait to hear what the guy had to say, but he knew what he hoped to hear.

The back door stood wide and the open car trunk had a fuck ton of Cannon's clothes inside. There were already suitcases in the backseat. The sight confirmed a growing suspicion Xan had. Cannon had been pulling away from work for months. Xan had wondered if Cannon planned to walk away. He had hoped, whatever Cannon plotted, those arrangements would include him. If they once had, it seemed they no longer did.

Xan moved quietly through the house. He followed the sound of shuffling. Xan found Cannon in the bathroom, tossing everything he owned into a duffle bag. He leaned his shoulder against the doorframe, blocking the way while waiting for

Cannon to notice him. Cannon finally turned and froze. Xan's stomach heaved. Cannon's eyes were dead but also red rimmed, as if Xan had broken him.

"Where are you headed?"

Cannon didn't respond.

Xan nodded. "I see. You don't have a plan. Did you have any intention of allowing me to explain, or were you just running?"

"Why would I let you explain? Everything that comes from your mouth is a lie." Cannon's voice sounded hoarse—like he had been screaming into the void.

"I wish I knew how to respond to that. You weren't supposed to find out."

Cannon snorted. "I'll bet. Is that how you justify everything in your mind? It doesn't matter if you live a complete lie with me, as long as I don't know it's not real?"

"Everything about us is real." Even Xan heard the rage in his voice. Cannon was not allowed to leave him.

Cannon's sad eyes were breaking him. "Like I said, nothing but lies, so why should I bother?" He moved to shove his way past Xan. Xan physically blocked him, prepared to do whatever it took to keep Cannon there. It didn't surprise him when Cannon punched him in the ribs.

Xan didn't react. While Cannon obviously hadn't held back, Xan had spent years being tortured to the edge of death. He could be a punching bag if that was what Cannon needed to forgive him. Cannon would fucking listen to him.

"When I told you I have no other option than the CIA, I wasn't joking. I traded one prison for another. At least, this one looks like freedom. Except when I failed to change your mind back at that cabin using reason, it was a failure nonetheless. I knew they would come for me, and they knew you would too. Because that's who you are, Cannon. You're a hero. The good guy. They needed you to remember it. If that meant I had to be tortured, then that was a sacrifice they were willing to make."

Cannon shook his head. "Why would I believe any of that? You're indispensable at the CIA. I'm easily replaceable at the FBI. No way would they trade you for me."

"They never planned to kill me, and they knew I could take whatever they dished out and be back to work on Monday.

But it has nothing to do with who can be replaced and you know it. It's about how much we've seen and know. You were enraged and causing noise. That was unacceptable. You're not dumb, Cannon. There's no way you didn't realize I was the person tasked with keeping you in line. I'd been trying for a while. What did you think would happen if I couldn't convince you to see things their way?"

"Congratulations. Hopefully, you got a raise for your performance. You absolutely had me fooled. But then again, I am a fool, so maybe it wasn't that hard to make me believe you genuinely loved me. Truly Oscar worthy."

Frustration welled in Xan's chest. "I do love you. Yes, I followed orders in that cabin, to an extent. But no one told me to kiss you that night or keep coming back for more. No one told me you would make me feel something no one else ever has before. That was you. It was me. You're perfect in every way to me. For me. This isn't fake. It's not an act. I love you. You have to believe me."

Cannon shook his head. "No. I don't."

Xan dropped his head and stared at the floor. Cannon tried pushing past him again and Xan let him go this time. He didn't know how to make Cannon see he loved him, but he was also beholden to the people who employed him. He couldn't force Cannon to see how much this hurt and how sorry he was for what he couldn't change.

Xan couldn't keep watching Cannon pack. It hurt too badly. "If I could choose, I'd always pick you. I never would've lied.

I'm sorry I wasn't free to make that decision. For what's it worth, I really do love you and I'm sorry."

Having said all he could, Xan headed back to his car. The moment he was behind the wheel and started the vehicle, his phone rang. Jake's name showed on the dash's screen.

Xan hit the phone icon as he backed from Cannon's driveway. "Hello?" Even he heard the defeat in his voice.

"Cannon resigned."

Xan's throat swelled. "I'm not surprised."

"You know we had plans for him."

With his elbow leaned on the door, and his arm holding up his head, Xan fought the urge to drive into the nearest tree. "I'm aware."

"So stop him."

"Go fuck yourself, Jake." Xan ended the call. When his phone immediately rang again, Xan tossed it out the window. He was exhausted and there was nothing left for him here.

CHAPTER ELEVEN

CANNON SAT BY THE fire pit and stared at nothing. Heat blasted his skin while Cannon stayed inside his head. He had thought he knew pain when he walked away from Knight, but that had just been weakness. Cannon had given everything to Xan. He had stepped out of the closet for him. Cannon would have done anything. The cabin he rented deep in the woods of Gatlinburg, Tennessee, felt cold and lifeless. He sought peace and found loneliness. Cannon supposed this would be the rest of his life now. Cannon needed to figure out where he was headed next. This was only a two-week rental. He couldn't afford to stay here forever. Cannon thought about continuing north. While he had been all over the world during his days with the special forces, he hadn't actually gotten to enjoy any of his travels. Not that he enjoyed himself now, either. Still, he couldn't go home. There was nothing for him there except memories of Xan every place he looked. As hard as he tried, Cannon couldn't forget how genuine and defeated Xan had looked before he left. He wished he knew what to believe. Cannon didn't want to keep being the fool. Yet thinking there was any chance Xan really loved him left him shattered and confused. Not that long ago, he would have given anything for Knight to let him prove himself. It murdered his soul to think of Xan feeling the same way. He just didn't have any fight left in him. Cannon was beyond exhausted.

"Why banjo country?"

Cannon didn't know why, but he wasn't surprised at all Royal had found him. He was more shocked he was the one who came. Cannon knew the bureau wouldn't let him walk away that easily. He never expected it to be Royal they sent. Maybe he should have, though. Royal would finally get to savor his dream of killing Cannon.

He lifted his beer bottle to his lips and took a drink before answering. "It'll make it easier for you to hide my body, I suppose."

Royal snorted. He pulled a lawn chair closer to the fire and sat. "It would if I cared enough to kill you."

Apparently, he was surrounded by liars. Still, he would entertain this. He had nothing else going on. "Why are you here, then? This is a long way to come for someone you despise."

"Yeah, well, I kind of like Xan and he loves you, so here I am."

Cannon didn't respond. He was tired of calling people on their lies. Cannon tossed his empty bottle onto the fire and popped open the cooler. "Do you want a beer?"

Royal shook his head.

Cannon twisted the cap off the bottle and threw it in the fire pit. For a minute, they sat in companionable silence while Cannon drank.

"You've surprised me with Xan," Royal said, breaking the silence. "One of the things I hated most about you was your cowardice when it came to Knight. But you openly claimed Xan, even with your family."

"I'd ask how you know that, but I'm sure you know everything."

Royal held his stare. "I do. I know way more than you ever will, and that's why I'm here. There's no way I can stay home and pretend I come from some rose-filled background and see the world as sunshine and butterflies. That's not who I am, and it's not who Xan is. When your parents stopped by the other day to ask Knight his thoughts on Xan, I thought, damn. He really did it. Cannon really grew some balls for Xan. Then you immediately ruined it."

Cannon rolled his eyes. "You obviously don't know as much as you think. Xan lied to me. He set up an entire fake operation to trick me into falling in line with the bureau. Excuse me if I'm not cool with that."

Royal cocked his head to one side and eyed Cannon. "Xan didn't set that up. Yes, he knew it would happen, but it wasn't his plan. They tortured him for real. He chose to let it happen because he could take it, and if he had said no, and he could've said no, you're who they would've tortured into submission. He wasn't okay with that. If you still can't see that he's not free, but he absolutely fucking loves you, then you don't deserve him. You deserve banjo country and to always look over your shoulder. You're not the victim in this story. If you leave Xan to clean up after you, I one hundred percent will think less of you than I already do."

Cannon rubbed his forehead. "I don't even know what that means."

Royal stared at him like he was dumb as fuck. "You saw what happened when you stepped out of line just a little. What do you think is happening now that you've fully thrown down the gauntlet?"

Cannon held Royal's stare. He didn't understand.

Royal slowly shook his head. "Oh, my God. You really are stupid." He blew out a slow, tired-sounding breath. "Well, I guess it's left to me, then. You might want to call Knight and say your goodbyes. Once I strike out against both alphabet companies, the two of us will have to run. You won't see him again."

"You'll have to take Knight and run? Seriously, what in the fuck are you talking about?"

It might have been the alcohol, but Cannon had never been more confused.

For a moment, Royal simply held his stare. Then, when he answered, he did so slowly, as if speaking to an idiot. "Xan is taking your punishment. If you don't get back to business, they'll likely kill him this time. They can't risk him joining you to strike out against them. You both know too much. It's a hell of a lot easier to make two people disappear than to cover up an entire media shit storm if either of you talk."

Royal might have been lying, but Cannon didn't think so. The guy hated Cannon. No way would he have agreed to help Xan bring him back. No matter how much Royal liked Xan, he loved Knight more. The truth was slow to penetrate his alcohol-soaked brain, but it hit like a truck once it struck. Xan was somewhere being tortured because of him. He remembered the defeat written on Xan's face. Cannon realized now the exact moment Xan had accepted his fate for letting Cannon go. Pain sliced through Cannon. Xan loved him. If he didn't, he never would have let Cannon leave, and Cannon absolutely knew Xan had let him.

"I hope you have a way to get us home. I'm in no shape to drive."

Royal smirked. "Don't worry about that. I have my ways."

Cannon stood and doused the fire. There was no time to waste. His baby was out there somewhere in pain. Cannon had some people to kill.

There were at least three broken ribs. Maybe more. He wasn't sure what these guys hoped to accomplish. Even if he believed for a second Cannon would answer his calls, what could he say? "Come back or these guys will kill me?" Cannon already thought he was a liar. Nothing he said would change a thing. Cannon was done. Soon, Xan would be dead, and Cannon would likely follow. Maybe they would toss Xan's dead body at his feet and force him to change his tune. Cannon was hardheaded, though. He might choose to die just to spite them, or for some holier-than-thou sanctimonious reason. Either way, none of it mattered anymore. Xan had nothing left but a lifetime of service without Cannon. That hadn't sounded so bad with Cannon at his side. After all, they had planned to give Cannon Jake's job. They would have had a newfound freedom. Without Cannon, and knowing the guy hated him, there was nothing now.

There was no blood in his arms. Tied above his head, he had lost feeling in them ages ago. He had no idea how long he had been here, but it felt like forever. Xan wished they would get on with it already. The physical pain was nothing, but the mental pain was a new torment he didn't know how to handle. He had found something and lost it. Now nothing mattered anymore.

The front door burst open, exploding inward as if a small detonation had taken it off the hinges. The three men they had spared for Xan's last days shot from the couch he had once shared with Cannon. The tiny safe house cabin didn't feel so safe any longer. At least, not for his captors, no doubt.

Cannon stepped through the door while smoke still somewhat kept him hidden. The men had been unprepared. The cabin was meant to be impenetrable by anyone not bureau-sanctioned. In a quick series of three pops, all three men went down with holes in the center of their foreheads.

Xan stared at the dead men with zero emotion. He had no hatred or pity. They had only been doing their jobs, and it was a deadly one. Cannon moved his way. Xan was too tired to lift his head.

"That's gonna be a lot of paperwork for you." He tried to chuckle, but it turned into a cough.

A knife appeared beneath his nose. "Take a breath. This'll hurt."

Xan didn't have time to question anything. The ropes holding his arms were cut away. His weight dropped and broken bones shifted. A cry tore from his lips with zero permission from his brain.

Then he was on the floor and in Cannon's arms.

Cannon rubbed his arms, trying to bring back the blood flow. Xan stared up at him from his lap. He would never get enough of seeing Cannon's gorgeous amber eyes.

"It won't take them long to come for us." He hated to point that out. Xan didn't know what made Cannon rescue him, but they both knew the property was heavily surveilled.

"No one will come for us."

Xan blinked. He was a little concerned he might black out. "I don't understand."

Cannon's closed expression gave nothing away. "I'm the only one who can give that order now."

Xan's heart fell. He knew how badly Cannon didn't want that director role and how much he would resent Xan for this. He glanced toward the nearby dead bodies.

Cannon kept massaging his arms. "They were fired."

Xan's eyes fell closed. Cannon was such a by-the-book guy. None of this was something Cannon could live with. They were still over, and Xan couldn't fix it. He deserved this pain.

Cannon's lips touched his gently, sparing Xan the pain from his cuts. "Don't pass out, baby. I can't carry you out of here without risking puncturing a lung. I can see your ribs shifting."

Xan could do this for Cannon. He would. With his back teeth gritted so hard he felt a crack, Xan rolled to his knees and pushed himself from the floor. Cannon moved with him, helping him out the door. It was a slow trek to the waiting SUV. Cannon had come for him completely alone. Xan didn't ask how Cannon knew where to find him. Like last time, they likely sent someone to fetch him. But it made no sense for him to be by himself.

"Why no backup?" It was all Xan could manage.

"Why would I need it?"

God. The cockiness. Xan was so in love with him. As Cannon helped him into the passenger seat, Xan breathed through the pain, but it made him weak and loosened his tongue. "I'm sorry. I'm so fucking sorry. You didn't want this life anymore and now you're stuck. Just leave me and run. If I'm dead, that buys you time to free yourself."

"Shut up, Xan."

Xan locked his back teeth. Cannon buckled his seatbelt for him. He paused and met Xan's stare. "I'll have you patched up and pumped full of drugs soon enough. Just hang on a little longer, okay?"

Xan managed a nod.

Cannon kissed him again. Then he pressed his forehead against Xan's. With his hand holding the back of Xan's head, he seemed to simply breathe Xan's existence for a moment. He kissed him again. "I love you. Just hang on." Cannon pulled away and closed the door behind him. Xan watched him circle the vehicle with his heart in his throat. He was scared as hell to hope, but he couldn't deny that was exactly what built in his chest. That might be the thing that killed him.

CHAPTER TWELVE

XAN SLEPT. HE SLEPT so long and hard, Cannon couldn't leave him alone for long. Cannon was scared as hell he would turn his back and Xan would disappear. He had to make him well. There was no other option. As much as he hated the idea of taking Jake's position, it was the only choice for him, and everyone knew it. They wouldn't have stopped at Xan. Cannon was no freer than Xan. If he hadn't returned, maybe it would have been his parents next. Then what? Maybe Royal and Knight just for shits and giggles. Who knew? At least if he was in charge, he could keep the people he loved safe. He could live with that. It wasn't like—at one point—he hadn't expected he would die a bureau man. Nothing had changed, except he had the man he loved. That was worth it. That was worth everything.

Cannon heard a noise in the kitchen and shot to his feet. He found Xan at the sink, getting water. His bare back was on display. Each time Cannon set eyes on Xan's scars, he was enraged all over again. He was mad at everyone, including himself.

Cannon moved to stand behind him and pressed his lips against one of the worst and deepest-looking marks on his back.

"I would've gotten that for you," he said against his skin.

"I know."

"You shouldn't be up."

"One thing I've learned the hard way is it's worse to stay still. Everything stiffens."

Cannon smiled against Xan's back. "I would've massaged you."

Just as he had been since he woke up the first time after his rescue, Xan didn't react to Cannon's flirting. It hurt Cannon's chest. He couldn't blame Xan for his anger. Cannon would be pissed too if he had been tortured twice for someone who didn't appreciate it. But Cannon's heart was still involved, and he couldn't take the distance.

His lips moved to another scar. He kissed Xan's skin. "Yell at me. Get it off your chest. I know I deserve it."

Xan turned. "You think I'm angry?"

Cannon didn't know how to respond with Xan's sexy blue eyes staring at him. He wanted to hide from the discussion that would likely end them. Cannon licked his lips. "Aren't you? I would be."

Xan's brow furrowed. "Why?"

Cannon made a helpless gesture toward his black and blue torso. "Because this is my fault. I'm supposed to love you and I left you to this."

"Did you know it?"

Cannon shook his head. He couldn't let Xan think that. "I'd turned in my resignation. There was no reason to believe they wouldn't accept it. Even if they hadn't, I never thought this would happen. I thought last time it was your plan."

Xan's eyes fell closed for a second. "I told you I was their property." He focused on Cannon again. "But no, I'm not angry with you."

Cannon felt like a kid as he shuffled from one foot to the other. "Then why are you shutting me out?"

"Because this is my fault." He set his glass aside. "I knew you had one foot out the door of the bureau, and because of me, they've pulled you back in. You're stuck, and it's my fault. You should've let them kill me."

Cannon wanted to shake him. "That's dumb, Xan, and you're not stupid. You know they wouldn't have stopped at you.

Who would they have taken next to force me to comply? They want me to know—good and damn well—I'm company property. There's no way they would've stopped at killing you and been like, 'Dang. That didn't work. Guess he really wants out. Let's pick someone else for the job.' They would've moved on to my dad and my mom. You'd be dead for nothing. This entire thing is my fault. I spent my entire career being the absolute best, following every order and solving every case. That was me. If I had tried to exist for any other reason, I wouldn't have stood out. If I hadn't buried myself in work to avoid dealing with my sexuality, then I would've been just another drone in the hive. I got myself into this. Worse than that, this is what I was aiming for. The director's position has always been my career goal. I just didn't know what was behind the curtain. I thought I was on the good side."

Xan chuckled. He grabbed his ribs like it hurt. "You are on the side of good. What does that tell you about how bad the bad side is?"

In a fucked-up sort of way, nothing else had made him truly understand the depths of Xan's childhood torture like that comparison. He shook his head. "I'm so goddamn sorry, baby." His voice cracked. "If I had known, I never would've let this happen to you. I don't give a fuck about the job. There's nothing I wouldn't do for the rest of my life to make sure you're happy and unharmed. You're worth more to me than freedom. If it wasn't you, they would've found some- one else."

Xan's eyes fell closed. His shoulders visibly drooped. He blew out a breath before he met Cannon's stare again. "I love you. There's no amount of pain I wouldn't endure to set you free. I told you lies. That's haunted me every day. You're right to hate me."

Cannon shook his head. "I don't." He made a helpless gesture. "Even before I learned you'd been taken again, I had already begun to question if I was wrong to walk away from us. I thought I knew what love was before I met you. Everything prior to us was just..." Cannon made another helpless gesture. He didn't know how to explain how no one had ever given him a reason to be himself and love freely. Lust and jealousy were his only driving factors before Xan. Then Xan had literally swept him away. "A life without you isn't worth living."

Xan took his hand and lured him closer. "Come here." He swiped his lips across Cannon's. Cannon felt the way Xan's body shook.

"You're shaking."

A tired-sounding chuckle escaped Xan. "I guess I'm getting old and can't handle torture the way I used to. My body feels weak."

Cannon grabbed Xan's glass. "Come on, sexy. Back to bed."

"I'm bored," Xan whined, but he let Cannon help him back to the bedroom.

"I'll stay with you. We can play footsie, since that's the only part of you that isn't bruised."

Xan grabbed his ribs again. "Oh, God. Don't make me laugh. It hurts."

Cannon's eyes unexpectedly filled with tears. It was the smallest thing, but massive to Cannon. Xan admitted weaknesses to him. Cannon couldn't imagine Xan ever doing that for anyone else. He was special to him. It was the most amazing feeling in the world. He would do anything to keep it.

With the TV playing in the background, Cannon did as he promised. His foot toyed with Xan's beneath the covers. A smile kept tugging at his lips and pulling at his cuts. It was worth it. Cannon was still his. He didn't resent Xan. Xan would keep searching for ways to untangle them from their invisible chains. He wouldn't let Cannon be trapped at the bureau forever if that wasn't what he wanted.

Still... "You know, you have a lot more power now and free time to spend with me. I can come to your office. We can lock the door." He waggled his eyebrows at Cannon.

Cannon laughed. "I'd already considered that. Maybe I could even use my pull to have you moved to my building. We could see how long it took for them to get tired of paying us to fuck on their dime."

Xan couldn't stop smiling. He was the happiest man alive with Cannon. Nothing mattered to him the way they did. "Will you marry me?" No one was more shocked by the question than him. Xan didn't take it back. "I know this proposal sucks and I don't have a ring or anything. But I love you, and I never want to feel the way I did when you walked away from us again. I want to know this is perma- nent."

"This is permanent."

Xan's forehead furrowed. "Was that yes?"

Cannon scooted closer. "Of course it was. Did you have any doubt? It's always been my intention to spend the rest of my life with you, so yeah. I absolutely will marry you."

Xan did his best to move closer and steal a kiss. Thankfully, Cannon took control and covered his mouth with his. Their tongues slowly played. Xan's stupidly exhausted body dug up some massive energy and stirred to life.

He groaned against Cannon's lips. "Damn. I want you to go shoot those guys again for making it impossible for me to make love to you right now. You always make me burn."

"Don't worry. I've got you." Cannon held his stare and slipped his hand inside Xan's shorts. He stroked.

Xan bit his bottom lip, fighting the urge to fuck Cannon's palm. "Jesus. This is torture. I want to move."

"Don't. Just let me have control."

He wasn't used to relinquishing power. Not anymore. Since leaving behind his past, he had always held a tight grip on every situation. Even while being tortured, he never let them have satisfaction. But he was putty in Cannon's hand. Cannon knew what he liked and used it against him.

"I want to watch you come."

A wicked-sounding chuckle fell from Cannon's lips. "I'll give you a show later. Right now, you're my only focus." Cannon was gentle with him, but effective. Xan sucked in steady breaths, concentrating hard on staying still while moving closer to the edge. The faster he blew, the quicker he could demand Cannon fuck a dildo while he watched. Xan wanted that. He desperately needed that. Pressure climbed his shaft. Xan whimpered. He was so close. Damn. He wanted to take his pleasure by lifting his hips and sawing in and out of Cannon's fist. Xan knew Cannon would stop if he tried. If

Cannon stopped, he would die. That was how close he was. His entire body tensed, sending shocks of pain through him. Xan didn't care. He wanted to blow. With his breath held, he focused everything on the pumping of his cock. Then his body jerked, making it feel like his ribs cracked again. It was worth it. Totally worth it. Ripples of ecstasy flowed through him, making him whine as Cannon pumped every drop of cum from his body.

"Beautiful," Cannon whispered, sounding enthralled by the sight of his orgasm. Xan knew the feeling. Cannon was his favorite show. He wanted to watch him for the rest of his life. Now was a good time to start.

CHAPTER THIRTEEN

A KNOCK LANDED ON Cannon's office door. A smile that felt evil stretched Cannon's lips. There were some perks to power. Cannon wasn't ashamed to enjoy them.

"Come."

Two men shuffled in, looking as worried as they should.

"You wanted to see us, Director?"

Cannon worked at keeping his emotions off his face. "Detectives Vaughn and Jones, have a seat."

The pair exchanged nervous glances and moved to fill the chairs across from Cannon's desk. They were night and day. One was fair in every way: light hair and eyes. The other was dark hair and eyes. Cannon picked a file from the stack on his desk. He moved as if to hand it to them before pulling back again. "Which of you stabbed my husband?"

The men visibly turned twice as anxious. Cannon practically felt them fighting not to look each other's way again.

Detective Vaughn swallowed. "Neither. It was Andy." He made a gesture as if searching for a way to continue. "You know, one of the guys who went missing a few months back."

The room fell silent as he eyed the pair. No one pointed out the obvious. Cannon was the one who made him disappear.

"We were following orders," Jones piped in, showing a lack of good sense. "At the time, we didn't know who we were taking. We were just told to take him to the warehouse and work him over before a team arrived to rescue Xan." He cleared his throat. "I mean, Special Agent Akim. We thought maybe it was some sort of loyalty test or training assignment."

Cannon nodded. Mindless drones. They might be useful someday. He held the file out. "I have a case for you two. A plane is already waiting."

Vaughn opened the file. His chin shot up. "Alaska?"

Cannon kept his expression clear. "Yes. Alaska."

"It's January."

Cannon didn't bat an eyelash. "People are murdered in January too. Are you refusing the case? I don't have a place for people who don't want to work."

The pair lost the battle against casting each other defeated looks. "No, Sir. Alaska is fine. I've always wanted to see the Northern Lights."

"Now is your chance to do it on the government's dime. The faster you go, the quicker you can get back." Cannon had more nightmare cases for the pair. He wouldn't fire them or kill them. If they lasted another year, maybe he would for-give them.

With their heads down, the pair headed for the door. When it opened, Xan stood on the other side. He moved aside and let them pass before stepping inside and closing the door.

Xan met his stare. "Oh, boy. Those were some defeated men. Did you fire them?"

Cannon chuckled. "Why would I do that when I can torture them instead? Legally, that is."

A sexy laugh fell from Xan's lips as he crossed the room. Cannon pushed his chair back enough to give Xan room to sit on the edge of his desk between Can-non's knees. "I think you're enjoying this position more than you thought."

Cannon ran his hands up Xan's thighs. "It definitely has its perks." He rolled closer. Cannon bit his bottom lip as he stared up at his sexy husband.

Xan groaned. "Don't give me that look. We have to meet your parents for lunch."

Cannon held Xan's stare as he worked on Xan's belt. "How much time do we have?"

A flush rose on Xan's cheeks. "Not enough."

"Doubting your ability, are you?"

Xan's expression turned sultry. "Do you really want your parents to walk in and see you getting railed?"

A laugh burst from Cannon. He was so in love with this man. There was no such thing as having him enough. Cannon ached for him every second of the day.

He popped the button on Xan's pants. "The door has a lock."

Xan jumped up and rushed to the door, turning the lock before returning to Cannon. Cannon laughed as Xan worked at getting him out of the bare minimum of clothing to get fucked. Even to his ears, he heard the happiness. A year ago, he had been fired and rehired. His life had been in shambles. He thought he had lost the love of his life, when really fate had been clearing the way for Cannon to find his soulmate. Cannon savored every kiss and touch they had shared. Every moan. Xan had enraged him and made him crazy. Yet Xan also completed him and gave him a life he hadn't dared to dream could be his. A year had changed everything for him. He couldn't wait to see what the rest of their life together had in store for him.

Gable's book will be the first in a new series, Atlantic City's Most Wanted, *Ruined*.

About the Author

CHARITY PARKERSON IS AN award-winning and multi-published author with several companies. Born with no filter from her brain to her mouth, she decided to take this odd quirk and insert it in her characters. One of her greatest loves is writing morally gray characters. You'll find them scattered throughout her hundreds of titles.

*Eight-time Readers' Favorite Award Winner

*2015 Passionate Plume Award Finalist

*2013 Reviewers' Choice Award Winner

*2012 ARRA Finalist for Favorite Paranormal Romance

*Five-time winner of The Mistress of the Darkpath

Connect with her online:

*Sign up for her newsletter: https://bit.ly/charityparkersonnewsletter

*Join her readers' group on Facebook: http://bit.ly/CharitysTribe

*Website: https://www.charityparkerson.com

*A list of her social media accounts and giveaways all in one place: http://hy.page/charityparkerson

CONTENT

CONTENT WARNING: DAMAGED DEVILS is a dark romance series that deals with dark subjects. There is murder, sexual assault, abuse, kidnapping, some dubcon, and power dynamic relationships. These are anti-hero books. They won't be for everyone.